IN SOMNIO

A COLLECTION OF MODERN GOTHIC HORROR

EDITED BY ALEX WOODROE

IN SOMNIO

A COLLECTION
OF
MODERN GOTHIC HORROR

EDITED BY
ALEX WOODROE

Dedicated to those precious voices who rose to tell us:

"I believe in you."

That is love, and we love you for it.

CONTENTS

A Note on Content Warnings

About the Creators

About Tenebrous Press

FOREWORD

by ANTONIA RACHEL WARD

"...the 'uncanny' is that class of the terrifying which leads back to something long known to us, once very familiar."
— Sigmund Freud, *The Uncanny* (1919)

A looming, many-roomed mansion, shrouded in night. It's the quintessential Gothic image. Ghosts haunt the hallways. Floorboards creak. *Something* lurks just around the corner. Something terrible, but also compelling. Mysterious. Like Emily St. Aubert in Ann Radcliffe's classic Gothic novel, *The Castle of Udolpho,* we both long and fear to glimpse the imagined horror that hides behind the veil. This is Gothic's enduring appeal: the mesmerizing darkness. The need to *know.*

Gothic literature first crept out of the shadows in the 1760s with the publication of Horace Walpole's *The Castle of Otranto.* Characterized by a sense of terror and uncertainty, the genre soon exploded in popularity, especially among women, who were the primary readers and writers of Gothic novels. In so many of the stories, heroines under psychological pressure continually question the evidence of their eyes and ears. Their imaginations run riot; they suspect horrors in the most ordinary of places.

In the Gothic, the familiar becomes terrifying. Twisted. Homes become prisons. Husbands, fathers, and lovers become potential murderers. Women are locked in attics, tormented by gaslighting, haunted by the memories of inhabitants who came before them. Sometimes their fears turn out to be founded. Sometimes they discover that it was all in their minds, after all.

But whatever the outcome, every Gothic story works as a journey into the secrets of the psyche; a revealing of that which must remain hidden in everyday life. The fears that are normally swept under the carpet rise to the surface, and as our heroines' sanity unravels, so do the structures that keep them in their place. For women, the Gothic becomes a genre of self-discovery; an opportunity to examine their true feelings. A safe realm of literature in which to realize, face, and ultimately defeat their fears.

The stories in this anthology will take you down frightening and difficult roads as the writers uncover the familiar darkness of the everyday. They will reveal the secrets and lies that simmer beneath the surface of ordinary life, and hold it under the light. You may be terrified, you may be disturbed, you may doubt the evidence of your eyes and ears, but like the heroines of yore, you will emerge stronger for the experience.

Antonia Rachel Ward is the founder and editor-in-chief of Ghost Orchid Press, a small independent publisher focusing on horror, Gothic, and supernatural fiction. Her short stories and poetry have been published or are forthcoming in anthologies by Silver Shamrock Press, Blackspot Books, and Orchid's Lantern, among others. Check out ghostorchidpress.com or antoniarachelward.com for more.

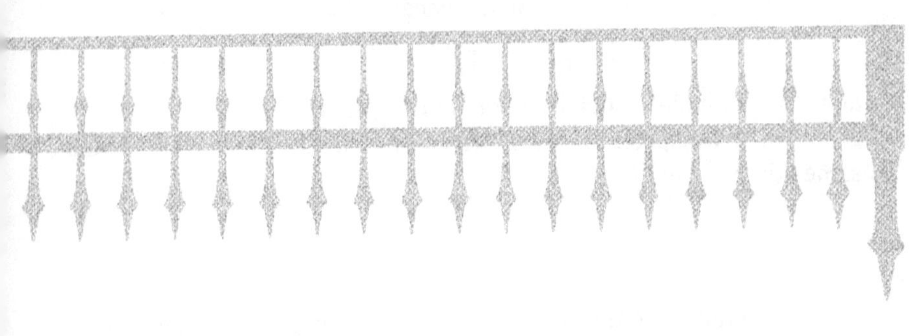

SENESCENCE

by J.A. BRYSON

The full moon shines creamy white, dissolving starlight like fine granules stirred in bitter tea. Sleep comes fitfully, disturbed by wind-whipped limbs rattling window panes, a steady scrape against the echoes of a murmuring sea.

I watch the sky brighten gray to pink.

I blink, lick the salt from my lips.

(I taste the same, I think.)

I press a finger to my throat, old skin stretched tightrope-tight—

Is this still me?

Am I—*right*?

***

A sable fan of hair spans in waves the adjacent pillowcase. A shoulder peeking from the sheets, the slope of sleeping lover's back. Pale nape of neck exposed but draped in silky black. How I ache to plant a kiss…

But no.

No.

Instead, I wait with baited breath.

I yearn for her to turn so I might better spy her tranquil face. I lean in close; I hope to catch a glimpse. If only she would stir, move an inch—a pinch—quick blink or sigh.

I'd whisper in her ear, "It's just a small change. We are the same still, you and I."

***

At dusk, we'd stumbled to the water's edge. Collapsing in the surf, our Naiad bed. She and I, limbs intertwined, impressing angels on the chill, wet sand. We'd probed the darkness, dampness, seeking—crying, shrieking—neither speaking. Knowing well, the rising tide would come and sweep our prints away.

A sentiment not meant to last.

A dream.

She took my hand. "I love you."

Moonlight streamed her cheeks.

I love you cannot sway how fate so neatly clears the letters from our fragile slate.

But we will last forever, you and I.

***

Lyrical the lashing, thrashing branches pound outside in rhythm with my lover's throbbing breast. I glance at the wooden chest, set upon the nightstand, propped open slightly, enough so wafting from inside the faintest air of formaldehyde. Therein, glistening on a needle tip, a luminescent pearl, a drip mingled with crimson.

A smile teases my swollen lip as I turn to watch her rest.

Oh, sweet angel, rest!

For surely, she could not protest an act of love so justified.

***

In grim reverie, I'd written my own eulogy: Here we have the scientist, fallen victim to biology. This dark fantasy I'd let simmer in my mind, those bygone sunsets we'd spent meandering the unraveling thread of sky and shore.

We'd walked with fingers interwoven like the fibers of my cap—a hand-knit woolen red—the jealous breeze conspiring to snatch it from my naked head. We'd seen gulls sucking the spattered guts of cracked crabs off the slatted walk.

    I'd said, "We are the guts, my love."

    And she laughed.

    The spectral taunting of her laughter ringing in my ears.

    We have no shells to keep us safe.

    We're sacks of meat, and nothing more—just sacks of meat more rancid with each passing year…

    A voice only I could hear chiding, reminding:

    "Your time grows near.

    Your time to say farewell to all that's dear."

    An incapacitating fear I no longer could ignore.

***

    Lab protocols were followed for my brute refute of my mortal station. Gown and booties, crisply donned. Mask and glasses, both put on. Blond wisps tucked inside a bouffant cap. Gloved hand. Squirming rat.

    Death comes by single snap, hard rap against the table's edge.

    A routine task of my vocation—to euthanize by dislocation.

    My final subject, how he differed from the rest. His red eyes focused, whiskers twitching; writhing, twisting in my fist. His skin— scaling and hairless. *Crustacean?* His substrate carpeted in a fresh shed fluff of downy white. I thought, perhaps I ought to make a wish before I break his neck. Or, at the least, a kiss goodnight.

***

    Now morning's blush behind the curtain thrills, excites and makes me certain. Light fills my veins and makes me flush. I hear the call of a hermit thrush, its haunting melancholic tune:

***

Oh, holy holy, ah
purity purity eeh
sweetly sweetly

***

But we will last forever, you and I.

So trill, so thin.
I feel it tingling on my skin as it begins to fissure.
Then—Ah!—the agony of splitting. Here I'm bursting; there I'm ripping. *My God!* Molars gritting. Blistering heat. My forehead sears; my hands (they hardly look like hands) my feet…?
I gasp. A rapid inhalation. Nerves scream in exhilaration.
I arch my spine—a tug, a tear. I bite my tongue.
A silent prayer.

***

I drift, at last.

***

Beneath the fresh-sloughed layers of my cast-off epidermis lies an iridescent sheen, a pallid bluish opalescence. It is tacky and elastic, stretching almost to translucence. And I cannot help but caress this flesh—a taction so exotic that the action is erotic.
Electric.
Spent, I gently roll to spoon my lover in a crescent moon.
I know she will awaken soon.

***

My love, I beg you not perceive my weak deceit a grieved transgression.
It is ours to share, this feat of biological ascension.
Love's dominion over fate, forever more, forever new
Liberated from senescence,
Is that not our greatest triumph—
Love's purest essence?
Ubiquitous telomerase expression
I've exploited just for you!

***

The faintest shift, the quaintest yawn, she blinks to greet the reddening dawn.

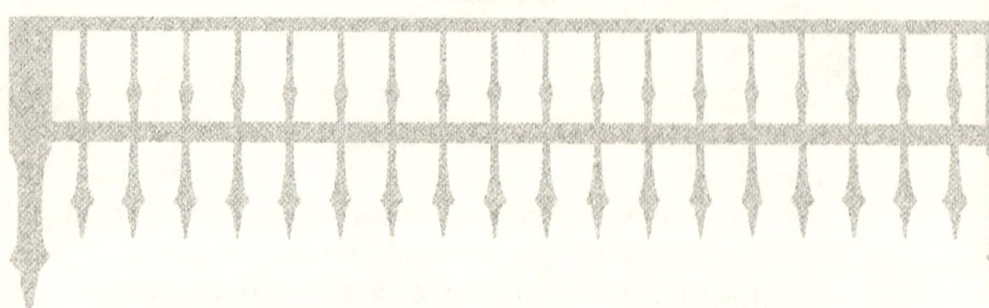

THE BLIGHT OF BLACK CREEK

by MARY RAJOTTE

Like a shadowy portent on the horizon, pruning season arrives at sunset. The way the last of the goldenrod catches those amber
beams and drinks them in like liquid gold is almost enough to help me
forget that as country folk, we're at the mercy of nature. But the shadows grow long, and when they stretch down the hillside, skimming
the edge of the village grove with needle-pointed claws, it's time to
choose.

The older neighbors—those who are too feeble or who suffer
from some ailment—sit under a canopy erected on the dirt road behind our house that marks the town limits. Watching the rest of us file
toward the grove, they clutch paper cups of steaming coffee they are
too nervous to sip, and they wait for the inevitable selection, one made
each year with careful contemplation. Sometimes I wonder if we'd
all be better off staying in the dark about such things instead of being
blighted by the decision.

Even though it takes twice the effort, Pa insists on coming
out with me. He crosses the road and uses his cane to help him hobble
across the sodden grass toward our plot, a long line of trees set apart
from the other single rows signifying each household in Black Creek.
I make it there first, taking the time to stop and let the feather-soft

leaves graze my fingertips, waiting until the deep perfume of musty soil whirls around me before I take up the tools and get to work. Pa appears just as I cut away branches to thin the crown on his tree.

"Here. Let me do that."

With his arms so gaunt that his sweater pools around him, he looks smaller than he ever has, so brittle that I worry a strong wind could lash him to ribbons.

I ignore his grasping hand and keep trimming. "You should go back with the others and stay warm."

"Nonsense. I'm not gonna sit by and watch with those geriatrics while decisions are made."

"It's not like that, Pa."

"Isn't it?" He nods toward Ethan Jones, who is a half yard away making notes on his clipboard for the Black Creek Council. "Leave me be now, girl. I'll tend mine and you do yours, like always."

He disappears on the other side of his tree, so I turn and use the lopper to cut away thicker branches from mine to help the sun and air circulate through the crown. With each snip, a dull ache thrums deep in my muscles, but it doesn't hurt much. It's something we've all had to get used to.

We're weeping willows, Pa and I. As far back as the Wilton roots go in this town, we've always been and for that I'm glad. The tree each family chooses is about the most important decision one can make.

Some go for tall, stately pines. Others pick oaks, whose trunks grow thick and sturdy. Each choice is decisive, spiritually binding our well-being to the tree planted for us at birth, so when I notice something in the dying light on my willow that shouldn't be there, my breath catches in my throat. Small brown spots sully the otherwise pristine, oval-shaped leaves. I hope it's just a beetle or some other nuisance, but it doesn't brush away when I reach up and sweep my thumb over it.

From beneath the boughs, everything goes quiet. Looking up at the crown, I find another leaf with the same discoloration. A sign of sickness, deep in the hardwood, like a lurking demon refusing to be exorcised.

Pa interrupts when he appears in the space between our willows. "Hannah, whatcha doing under here, huh?"

When he parts the sweeping branches to join me, I can't hide my expression and when he sees what I do, he cups his hand against my cheek.

"It'll be fine, hon. Everything's gonna be alright now."

Before I can think of what to say, he takes the lopper, cuts away the branch, and crumbles the leaves to dust.

"Over here!" he shouts before I can stop him. "We got some trouble over here, Ethan."

Panic flushes across my chest, rooting me in place. But Pa moves out from under the tree and goes beside his own. Ethan is there to meet him when I emerge.

"Whatcha got here, Roy?" Ethan asks.

Pa holds out his lantern close to a soft spot on his willow and nudges it with his cane. The bark sinks in and then crumbles away.

"Oh," Ethan says, kneeling to inspect the trunk. "Well, that's not good now, is it?"

He pokes his pencil at the soft wood and then encircles it in small insect holes that sully the beautiful peaks and ridges of the bark. He scribbles a moment on his clipboard and then glances up at Pa. "Aw, hell I'm sorry, Roy."

When Ethan lifts his lantern, it etches the faces of the others gathering behind him with regretful relief. As he ushers them away, I move beside Pa.

"You can't, Pa."

"It's done," he says.

The further Ethan plods, the more my stomach churns. If I tell him what I found on my willow now, he'll know I hid it. I should have been brave enough to say something right away.

Behind Pa, more than a dozen old willow stumps cut and left to whither are remembrances of how much we'd lost over the years, but it's the closest one, my big brother Robbie's stump, that hurts so much. And no matter what I do or don't, no matter what I say or keep to myself, I'm still losing Pa for good, making me the last Wilton in Black Creek. Keeping quiet is like a betrayal to Pa, and that's not a thing I can live with.

I turn to chase after Ethan, but Pa plants his cane in front of me.

"Leave it be, Hannah."

"But—"

"Should they strike us both down?"

"Pa…you saw, same as me. It's only a matter of time now that there's scab on my leaves. I gotta tell them."

Pa clamps his hand around my arm and yanks me toward him, gritting his teeth and bulging his eyes wide. "This been a long time comin', no matter how bad you wanna wish it away."

"But, Pa."

"Hush now. Just hush." He loosens his grip but doesn't let go. "You going after Ethan won't fix things. Stop being so headstrong like you always been and listen to me, girl."

He tries to smile, but his blue eyes are tinged with such sadness that I have to look away.

"I'm an old man, Hannah. You know as well as I do my clock's been ticking down these last few months. But that don't mean we both gotta go."

I shake my head and turn, blinking back tears. "They'll see my tree at some point, Pa. Maybe not now, but someday soon. It's just a matter of time, like you said."

"Don't you say that." He spins me to face him. "You can go to the city. Find a new doc that don't know us or anything about this place. He'll figure out what's wrong. Treat you. Make you better before anyone else is the wiser. You *will* do this, Hannah. For me. You hear?"

His eyes are wild and glazed. When I nod, he lets out the breath he's been holding and pats me on the shoulder before he turns to face the others standing a few yards away in conversation. I already know what they're saying. How they're planning the examination. It's all so callous, him having to watch, to listen to them pore over every last inch of his tree looking for rot, but I know what he's doing. He's not a glutton for punishment. He's looking after me, even now, even with what he's facing, not just tonight but in the coming weeks. Giving me time to brace myself for life without him.

We've lost so much and here we are, us Wiltons, blighted again.

The men gather their lanterns and flashlights, speaking in hushed tones, arming themselves with loppers and pruners. Every muscle in my body aches with the urge to fight them back. I stand behind Pa, my hand on his shoulder to steady him as he sits stoic in his chair. Next to his feet, his satchel of tools waits. I reach in and take a small knife before anyone notices.

Next to our grove, Mama's tree stands in line with the rest

of the May family. Losing her broke me but at least I still have some place to hear her whispers, still catch her lingering spirit, one that left too soon. With dark brown bark that's etched with grooves, her hawthorn's deep-toothed leaves have gone gold and curl up at the edges, and her red fruit has turned dark and ripened with the season.

"You got the best of both me and your Pa in you, Hannah," Mama told me when she took a turn for the worse. "Your strength? That's from your Pa. But that fire in you? That's from me. It'll help you fend off any threat. Don't you forget that."

I leave Pa to stand under her tree, smoothing my hand over her branches. Deep inside, some remnant of Mama still lingers, and I know it's her willing me to do what I have to do to protect myself. To carry on.

I use the knife to slice off a healthy length of the branch closest to me. A strong smell like ammonia wafts from the cut end. I peel off my thin scarf and wrap it around the branch, then shove it in my pocket before I turn back to where Pa waits.

Back at our willows, Ethan's son, Jacob, sets a work light between the trunks. When our gazes meet, his eyebrows knit together in the middle with concern. I try to nod, to signal I'm okay, but I can't. I'm not.

The choking sputter of the generator pierces the quiet before it grumbles to life, spewing out a noxious cloud and shining a harsh spotlight on Pa's tree. One side is bare, the bark having sloughed off like dead skin. It lays in the grass like a scab, dried and brown. Orange spores with feathery bronze hairs sully the roots. Ethan steps over downed branches and crouches so he can press his fingertips to the trunk. He picks up some fallen leaves and examines them under his small headlamp, making a note about the discoloration.

As he cranes his neck to get a better look at the other side, he snaps his fingers. Jacob repositions the light so it shines where Ethan points. I edge my way around the tree to see splotched hard mushrooms scattered up the trunk.

"Y'see, there's nothing we could'a done, Hannah," Pa says. "Rot's clear through. Sickness seething from the inside out."

As Ethan takes out a poker and pries at the roots, I turn away. Out near the road, folks linger, shuffling from one foot to the other, waiting for a final declaration. I start toward them, my hands balled into fists at my side.

"Why don't you all go on home now, huh?" I shout.

"Hannah!" Pa calls out behind me, but I keep going.

"There's no need for y'all to sit here watching."

When I make it to the road, the older ladies are packing up and heading off to their homes, but most still linger, keeping their eyes averted.

"This isn't entertainment or about the good of the town. This is about *my* family," I say. "Us Wiltons have been the ones to take this burden on more than anyone else here."

"Come now, Hannah," Jacob says, approaching. He grabs my hand, but I tear it away. "They ain't out here to make light of what you're going through. This concerns everyone in the village, you know that."

I spin toward him, hot tears making his face blur and the shadows of the grove seep into him like ink stains. "That don't mean it isn't cruel, them sitting here with their popcorn and coffees like its Sunday down at the drive-in."

I try to brush past him, but he grabs my arm. "I know. And I'm sorry. I really am."

The way his voice breaks is too much for me so I pull away, rushing back to where Pa sits alone. By the time I get there, Ethan's already giving his diagnosis.

"If it were just the scab, or the crown gall on its own, it'd be one thing, Roy. But to have both? No one can come back from blight like that."

"I get it. You're just doing what you gotta, Ethan." Pa struggles to his feet. He stumbles a few steps sideways and I catch him before he falls over into the soft grass.

"I'm fine, Hannah. Leave me be."

He pats my hand and then brushes it away, not out of embarrassment but pride. The way he moves toward the house, each step calculated, shows he's accepted his fate but won't let them get started until he's good and ready.

They wait until the screen door taps against the doorframe behind him. When it does, Ethan turns to the men and nods.

When they come with their axes and chainsaws, one of them driving a wheelbarrow with a bucket of herbicide, my blood boils. They do it like this so it's quick and painless for them. If I had my say, they'd be forced to do it the old way, with a two-man saw. Sweating, aching, their hands blistering hot by the time they get through the trunk and expose its rings and the dark core wood.

It would be easier for them if I left like Pa's done. But I want them to suffer. Wood chips and bark at my feet. Sawdust raining down on me like snow. They deserve to see it all, to look into my eyes when they raze this willow. To witness my defiance when they open that bucket of chemicals and work to keep the trunk from sending up shoots before it dies completely. But that won't rid them of me. I'll be standing right here.

Some of them stay on the ground, firing up the chainsaws. Others climb ladders to cover all sides, cutting the branches that are closest to the ground first, and then razing what's left. When they're done, they practically trip over themselves to paint the stinking poison mixture on the stump, smoothing the gunk across the lighter rings of sapwood and all over the remaining bark with all its nooks and crannies. I willfully catch each of their gazes so they can see what this does to a person. And when they're gone, and only the woodsy smell of sawdust perfumes the air, above me, the soft muttering of wind through the leaves is Mama's voice lilting toward me.

"That fire in you to fend off any threat? That's from me. Don't you forget that."

With the others gone, I waste no time doing what I must. Something I heard Pa whispering to Mama when she took ill. An unspeakable act, one that goes against the order of things here in Black Creek. Something that no one's ever had the gall to try. But I might, if it'll save me.

With Pa's knife in hand, I go to my willow and, beneath her canopy, carve out a notch in the bark at the v-shaped joint closest to me. Electric pain shoots through my nerves, but I ignore it and take out the cut branch from Mama's hawthorn. It sits so nicely in the incision, as if it belongs there. Using some twine snuck from Pa's workbag, I secure the branch to the trunk with a knot the way he taught me when I was a young girl helping him tend to our grove. Then I sink down onto my knees, my cheek pressed to the cool, rough bark, alone out here, as close to Mama as I'll ever be, with only my lone willow tree to show Black Creek us Wiltons were ever here.

***

Two days after the men inflict their treatment, Pa's health worsens. He takes to the bed and doesn't talk much anymore, preferring to spend most of the time he's got left sleeping.

I'm standing outside his room, listening to the rattle in his throat when I get a knock on the front door long after dinnertime. When I go to see who's calling so late, Jacob appears on the opposite side of the window through Mama's lace curtains. My stomach drops. I pull my sweater tight around me, opening the door only a crack. When I see he's alone, I swing it wider.

"Sorry to call on you unannounced," he says, peering around me. "Wanted to see how you're doing. How's your Pa holding up?"

I brace myself against the door frame. "He stopped eating a few days ago. Refuses to drink. Won't be long now."

"So, Hannah," Jacob says.

I hold up my hand to him, but I don't look. I can't. I'll break down if I look in his eyes again. "Just tell me how. How are they going to do it? Burning?"

He doesn't answer at first. The floorboards creek underfoot as he shifts.

"With the rot, everyone's afraid it could spread through the grove," he finally says. "We don't got time to wait for the stump to dry out before that."

"So, they're going to uproot it then?"

"Hannah," he says, so soft I almost think I imagined it.

Outside, a motor revs and I spin, my eyes wild with panic. And I see it in his red-rimmed eyes.

"You know how it is with rot, Hannah," he says, wringing his hands. "How it can stay in the soil for so long."

I rush to the window where the scene outside catches my breath. Ethan barks orders at a man suited in protective gear and a face shield, who moves what looks like a lawn mower toward the Wilton copse. When they start to grind away at the corewood of Pa's willow, I cry out at the brutality and spin away so fast I have to catch myself from collapsing.

Then it clicks. Pa.

I bolt down the hall to his room, but when I get there, he's already fading. Tendrils of his hair lay on the pillow around his head like wilted leaves. Blood trickles from his nose. His lips have gone bone dry like desiccated bark. I collapse to my knees and take his hand in mine.

Gone is Pa's warmth and strength. Gone is his color, now blanched away. Torn from him without care, the only connection he's got left to this place, to me, is gone now, too. With nothing left to root him here, he becomes untethered and drifts away to that other place where Mama and Robbie are waiting.

When the motor outside finally falls silent, I bury my head in the crook of Pa's arm. My tears fall hot like a summer storm, stirring up his moldering scent, but I take it in as a reminder of him. When the rattling in his throat quiets, I gather him toward me to catch some remnant of his gentleness, but he is all sharp angles now that the life has seeped from his core. And like the breeze high in his willow tree on a late fall night, he shushes and sighs, giving up his last breath until he falls forever still.

When the grinder starts again outside, I bolt up. That whirring sound needles the back of my neck and I scramble from Pa's room and stagger to the front door where Jacob remains. He's got his hat in his hand now, his eyes cast downward.

"It's the only solution," Jacob says. "To stop the rot. We need to remove the others to make sure. You understand that, right, Hannah? How the fungus can travel from one to the other? It's for the good of us all."

I glare up at him so fiercely he jolts back away from the door so I can pass. A woodsy haze hangs over the grove, prickling my nose.

A gaping hole where Pa's willow once stood stares up from the ground like an open wound. Piles of sawdust sit like pulverized bones in wheelbarrows, which the men fill up and haul away. But they aren't done.

The man working the grinder moves toward Robbie's stump and steadying himself, he lowers the machine a few inches at a time, swinging it from side to side so it shaves away what remains bit by bit. I let out a scraping howl, but the machine is like a hideous beast that swallows my voice whole. Seeing this carnage, that what remains of us Wiltons is nothing more than mulch, deflates me. I stagger toward my tree, each step a battle, but I refuse to let them see me falter. Secreted away under her canopy, I lean forward and press my palm to her, hoping to absorb her strength, but my hand squishes in something soft and when I turn it over in the dim light, rotting bark stains my skin.

...with only my lone willow tree to show Black Creek we were ever here.

Shaking and nauseated, I go to where I grafted the hawthorn branch. Shoots from the willow poke from the cut spot. The hawthorn and willow didn't have enough contact with each other. They haven't had a chance to meld.

Air shushes on my face and in the tiniest moment of hope, I imagine it's Pa somehow. Instead, Jacob returns to the place where, on so many warm summer nights, he spoke with that golden shimmer in his green eyes about dreams bigger than our lives in Black Creek. That shimmer is gone now when he sees the panic in my eyes. The rot on my hand.

When Jacob reaches for a branch and snaps off a twig like a bone, I wince. When he crumples the frond, it knocks the breath right out of me. Then he stops. He sees it, the smooth grey hawthorn branch, how it doesn't match, how it's somewhere it doesn't belong. He pauses, reaching up and grazing his fingers over the cut end where it fights to wed with the willow.

"Damn it, Hannah," he says, teary-eyed. "You always gotta be so stubborn, don't you? Always doing things without thinking about them first."

When he turns and leaves the safety of our hiding place, I'm sure he's calling the others to come for me. I lean against the trunk, feeling the sturdiness in the corewood, and tilt my head back, getting lost in the graceful sway of branches at night one last time before I face up to what I've done.

I reach out and touch my fingers to the spot where the willow and the hawthorn meet and it's like I'm holding onto Mama's hand and Pa's too, both at the same time. But then Jacob returns. I thrust out my hands like a woman condemned, but instead of dragging me away, he takes out tape and wax and gets to work sealing the wound so the branches can marry.

"You can't," I say, reaching for his hand. "This is my burden. Not yours."

"It's done," he says, securing the branch with the tape to hold it in place.

"I didn't think, is all. I acted rash. After Pa, after what he found—"

He pockets the tools. "It's done now. I'm not gonna let your efforts go to waste."

"But the trees. They're too different. It might be all for nothing. And if they find out. If they see what I've done—"

"What *we've* done."

The thought of it makes my stomach sink, but he takes my hand and leads me out from under the canopy.

"We just gotta have faith that it'll take." He leans down until we're eye-to-eye and a tiny golden shimmer of hope sparks to life beneath the worry. "That the hawthorn will help you heal. And then come spring, your willow will bloom into something new. Something better. Stronger. And we can forget about this blight for good."

***

Weeks pass slow and wearisome, but when the first buds peek from their hiding places across Black Creek, there's a knock at my door and I'm sure it's Jacob ready to see if what we've done has worked.

I pull my coat closed before I open the door where I find Ethan waiting.

"You're needed in the thicket, Hannah."

I peer around him. It's like the equinox all over again, with half the town watching, their gazes making me feel like a caged animal on display.

"Why's that?" I ask, keeping my hand cinched around the scarf at my throat.

"Come. Now."

I peer around him. "Where's Jacob?"

"Just come with me, Hannah. Everyone's waiting on you."

I swallow hard when he moves aside, but I go out onto the veranda. I take the steps slowly, making sure I wrap my scarf tight before I make the short walk to where my lone willow proudly boasts small pinkish-white blossoms peeking from her branches.

I gasp at the sight of such vitality amongst such starkness. Unable to stop myself, I rush toward Jacob, who stands staring up at her with his mouth hung open.

At the place in the joint where he grafted the hawthorn, its smooth, grey bark has darkened into a shade of brown. Deep ridges extend along the branch where it has fused to the grey willow, roughly furrowed and spiked with tiny thorns like cat's claws.

"*This*," Ethan says, stepping forward and reaching for the foreign branch, "is an *insult* to every family in Black Creek. There are rules. A pact every one of us must abide by."

When he glares at me, my willow-like stature inspires me to tilt my head high.

"To cheat our traditions in this way, Hannah? Well, we have no other choice."

He snaps his fingers, calling forth a team of men waiting near the grove.

"No, dad! You can't do this!" Jacob shouts, cutting off the group, but when they ready their chainsaws, I move in front of them, wrapping my arms around the trunk and interlocking my fingers.

"Move away," Ethan says.

"I won't let you just uproot us all."

"We have rules here, Hannah. Tradition. What you've done is a slap in the face. Once we're done here, we'll tend to your Mama's tree, too."

"Mama's tree isn't hurting anyone. There's no blight in her hawthorn, or else you would have cut it down when she passed."

"That was for your Pa's sake. We should'a put her tree down then but we kept it up. For him. 'Cause we knew the toll her passing took on him. But who's to say it wasn't her that passed some sickness on to his tree? And Robbie's?"

"I won't allow you to just erase us like we never existed!"

"Enough of this now, Hannah! This is how its gotta be!"

He grabs for my collar, but his hand catches on something. He gasps and jerks backward. Pinpricks of blood stain his fingertips. His brow furrows, wrinkling his forehead rough like bark, but he grasps for me again, this time tearing away my scarf.

Encircling my neck, rows of tiny black thorns protrude from my skin, stretching up to my chin in a studded armor.

Ethan bolts backward. "Jesus H! What the hell is that?"

Behind him, some others come toward us, holding their tools and workbags at the ready. Pushing past them, Jacob studies me for a moment then reaches out, stopping short of touching his fingers to the barbs.

"It worked," he says, a relieved smile spreading across his face. "Didn't I say? Didn't I tell you to have faith that it would take?"

"You did this, son?" Ethan says. "You helped her with this desecration?"

Before Jacob can respond, Ethan shoves him aside and lung-es at the tree. His skin snags and slices open on the newly-sprouted thorns. He lashes at an offshoot from one of the branches. With a de-cisive snip, he shears it free, sending pain shooting up my fingers. He turns back for another attack, but a thorny willow branch slices his cheek, drawing a thin thread of blood to the surface. Raising the machete, he hacks away the barbs stretching from the base of the tree high into the canopy.

Clutching at the searing pain that seizes my neck, I scream and spin away. Echoing my agony, my tree slashes a branch through the air, catching Ethan in the eye, forcing him back with a howl.

Cowering, he calls to the other men gathered at the road. Whis-pering and gawking, they edge toward my willow, scampering back when the tree bends with a deep groan. Thrashing her spinule-studded branches at those who get too close, she flogs them until they retreat. Ignoring their gaping stares, I move near, placing my palm flat against her, to marvel at what she's become, how she's protected me, healed me.

When I sigh, my breath calms her, stirring her blossoms and rustling her leaves. In her canopy, there are no spots on the new leaves. Her branches spread strong and wide, and her roots lodge deep within the soil. But she is changed. She sways with an air of enchantment now, one that emanates from her barbed and knotted trunk. She has strength, like Pa, to take on any challenge. The fire of my Mama, to face any threat. And coursing deep within the corewood, my spirit. One that's not blighted, but resilient.

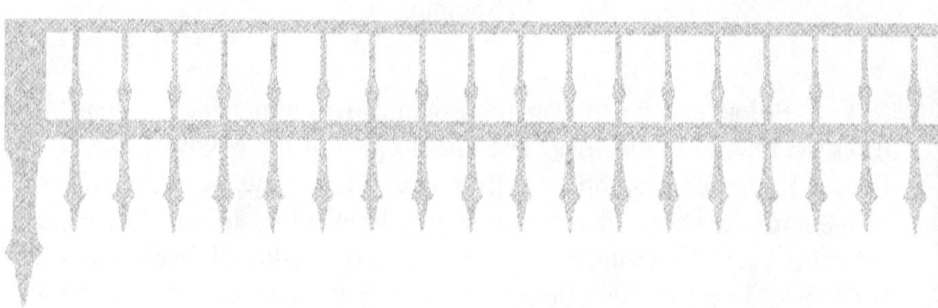

TRESPASS

by ASTER S. MONROE

i
Mama used to say that there are things in this world so heavy with sadness that it clings to them, and people like us can feel it, even after years and years, like the way you feel somethin that you're reaching towards but it's snatched away at the last minute.

Mama was sad. She had sadness in her skirts and sadness in the lines of her face. I guess I grew up with it, so it's almost like coming home, in a way, findin somethin that feels like her.

Now.

You say that I'm a witch, and I'll say that you're right. But you're not a man no more and you don't own this tree, you just haunt it.

Naw, there's no law under God or man that says you own a tree just by haunting it, so if you don't wanna help me out, you can just git.

ii
I don't like skirts and I ain't afraid of hard work, and you ain't even alive, so no, I don't think it's any of your damn business how high I hike up my dress.

Now if you were a real gentleman, 'stead of a nosy ghost, you'd help me so I don't have to dig up the whole goddamn tree to find your bones.

Thought so.

iii

You know what I'm afraid of? Dogs.

Our neighbor had a fearsome bitch—something in its life had bred that thing *mean*. When I was real young, I had to walk by that thing every day to and from school, and it would jump at the fence at me like it wanted to tear me limb from limb.

Then one day—an' I remember this as clear as a bell—three things happened. First, the sky dawned so blue that it made your teeth *ache* to look at it. Second, little Tommy Steeler got his hide tanned for spittin tobacco in the schoolyard. Third, my neighbor left his front gate unlocked.

You ever been attacked by a dog, Johnny?

It's like bearing down a storm. I couldn't do *nothin* but stand there as it lunged at me. I don't remember much afterwards, but I remember standin there, every single one of my muscles seizing up, locked-frozen outta fear.

That dog tore the meat right off my bones, from shoulder to elbow, and chewed around my ribs something fierce. If I weren't a lady, I'd take off my dress 'n show you. It's a mighty ugly scar.

That's why I ain't afraid of you, Johnny. Don't take it personal—I ain't afraid of anything but angry men and angry dogs, and you ain't even a man no more.

The dog? Well the day after, it started hacking up blood and died all twisted up in our neighbor's yard. I didn't see it, on account of being in the hospital, but my aunt told me all about it when she brought me a basket. I still remember that supper in the steel bed—hot bread and

You say that I'm a witch and I say that you're right. But you're not a man no more and you don't own this tree, you just haunt it.

cold chicken, peaches from a can. I could only eat with one hand and made a right mess of myself.

My neighbor, of course, was spittin mad. He told the sheriff my aunt had fed that dog meat with ground glass in it, but no one could ever prove it.

There's witches for ya.

iv

See, Johnny, right here in the grimoire. It says, "knucklebone of a wrongly kilt man", an' that's what you are.

Ya, so the spell is to kill a man, what of it? I don't rightly think you can judge *me*, Johnny Weir, considern the circumstances of yer death.

You may be wrongly kilt, but you ain't wrongly judged.

v

What'd I tell you before, Johnny? I ain't scared of the dark.

It just makes it harder to see where to dig.

I gotta come later now, since Aunt Tabby's started getting all suspicious-like about my "after-school" activities. There's some gang of boys tearin up things 'round town—mailboxes and girls. Shassie from school had a run-in with them and it wasn't pretty.

Aw, Johnny. Lookit that scowl. Almost think you're worried about me. Is that what it is, Johnny? You gettin fond?

Well, save it. I can take care of myself just fine. And it's not like you'd be any help in the state you're in.

Oh!

Look! See those pretty little things floatin just beyond the trees? Mama called em ghost lights. There's wicked souls in those lights, an' they lead good people off their God-given path to sin.

Mama knew everything about everything. I listened as hard as I could, but she still didn't get to tell me all she knew before she died. They buried her stories with her, and I think they're still there now, nestled in her bones with the grubs n' worms.

Yep, this tree, too. Oh Mama had *stories* to tell about this tree. See, back when she was a girl, an' these lands were wilder, they used to call this the Hanging Tree. Fer reasons you could imagine, I suppose. They hung a man here who shot a banker an' two of his clerks over a deal gone wrong. Toby LaGrange, his name was, 'n they say, on cold nights like this, you can still hear him cryin as they put the noose 'round his neck.

Ha, here I am tellin ghost stories to a ghost.

You had to know about the stories too, I'm sure. After all, you picked this tree to die under, and I don' think *I'd* ever pick a place to die that had no history.

Aw, Johnny, don't you go and get so *huffy*, I was only sayin the truth.

vi

What's it like bein a ghost, Johnny?

I don't suppose I'll ever know, myself, on account of the fact I got no soul.

No witch has a soul, Johnny. They all belong to the devil, who keeps 'em in a glass jar down in Hell. Or so I've heard.

Mama sold my soul when I was just a baby—needed it for a spell to bring back my daddy, but I don't think it worked.

Or maybe it did, but she killed him dead again real soon. Aunt Tabby says they never really did get along, even before I was born. Went at each other like alley cats, she said, 'though I don't think I was supposed to hear that conversation.

My mama loved my daddy, though, I know that.

It's why the sadness chased her 'round like a hound dog for the rest of her life. She would've brought him back a thousand times, if she could, but she just had me.

Sometimes I wonder what kind of man my father was. Not a very smart one, I imagine, marrying a woman with no soul.

vii

I don't think I could ever be a ghost, even if I *did* have a soul.

I dunno, don't you think it's just *sad*, walkin 'round this same old tree again and again and *again* for the rest of forever?

Mama was like a ghost in her last years, just floatin around the house, not seein nothin. I'd never wanna live like that, my skirts dragged all heavy with sadness.

When my time comes, I'm gonna take the devil's arm as pretty as you please, step down to Hell with my head held high.

Well *I* think you're a real coward, Johnny Weir. What do you think yer doin here, other than avoidin yer responsibilities? *Men* don't run 'n hide and cling to their mama's skirts 'cause they're afraid of facin St. Peter's judgment.

One way or another, God is coming for you, Johnny, and yer doin yourself no favors by pretending you didn't ruin no lives.

viii

I've almost dug 'round this whole tree, Johnny, so you might as well tell me. I'm gonna find your bones sooner or later, an' yer not helping yourself any by being so pinch-lipped about it.

Fine, have it your way. I don't know why yer being so goddamn *diff'*cult.

I bet you think I wanna kill this man out of *jealousy* or some petty love-sickness. Well, you don't know nothin about me, Johnny, and you don't know *nothin* about women. I know you think yer girl June sold you out to the sheriff an' that's why they gunned you down, but that don't mean you gotta take out her sins on *me*.

Johnny, I—

Johnny

Johnny yer scarin' me.

ix

Bet you thought you were rid of me.

Aw, Johnny. I suppose I'm sorry too. Should've guessed yer girl would be a sore point for you. Aunt Tabby says that I'm like a bulldog sometimes, grabbin onto something and not lettin it go even when it ain't none of my business.

Now, Johnny.

I'll say that I never told you a lie in my whole life. Even about the kinda spell I wanted to cast with yer bones. So you can trust me when I say that I promise I won't ex-or-cise you from your restin place. I promise I'll leave yer bones be, and you can keep haunting this sad tree as long as you'd like.

I promise.

x

Right over that hill? You sure?

This better not be a trick, Johnny, otherwise you'll be answerin to my shovel.

xi

I can't say, Johnny, only God can judge our souls.

Fer what it's worth, I think you can be a good man even though you've done bad things.

Dunno if that's enough to get you into heaven.

xii
I ain't a good witch.

I don't think any witch can be *good*, even Aunt Tabby who goes to church every Sunday an' bakes peach pies for our pastor. Her soul's still in that glass jar in hell, bangin around an' making Lucifer's music.

But I think maybe—

A witch could try her hardest not to be bad?

Killin a man ain't *good*, but if I kill a bad man to save good people, then maybe I won't be quite bad either.

But I'd rather be bad than do nothin. I'd rather sin, so good people don't have to. My soul's already lost, an' theirs is not.

I think sometimes that I was born to be a sin-eater, to keep the bad secrets of other people an' swallow their sadness. Just like with my mama, 'cept I couldn't save her.

I tried to swallow all the sadness in her soul, but she still got drowned in it.

I think about her near every day.

xiii
I don't ever wanna be sad, Johnny.

I wanna walk around sad places, feel the thickness of their circumstances an' drape it 'round me like a cape to keep me warm. I wanna talk to sad people—and sad ghosts—to find out what in their soul makes 'em so heavy. I think sad people have hearts like overripe fruits, 'n they just need someone to come along and pluck it from their chests.

But Johnny, I don't ever, *ever* wanna be sad.

xiv

Johnny—

I ran here from school, Johnny, Mr. Myer is gonna be *so mad* when he finds out, but—

I needed to tell ya what I found out.

Now, Johnny, you gotta promise not to become angry like you did last time, *swear* on yer grave that you won't, otherwise I ain't gonna tell you a thing.

Alright.

Now I asked Aunt Tabby 'bout yer girl June and she wouldn't say nothin, which was strange if June had run off with the sheriff's boy or somethin like you were spoutin' off about—

Johnny, I swear to Heaven that if you don't knock off that angry, hateful glare, I'm gonna march right home and you ain't ever gonna find out what happened to June.

Yeah, you calm right down, now.

Where was I? Aunt Tabby was close-lipped, so I hadta go to the oldest gossip I know, which is Millie from the Corner Store. She'd tell ya anythin for a tray of sweets, only they have to be soft, see, on account that she has no teeth.

I hadta take Aunt Tabby's lemon bars for the church bake sale, but Millie told me *everythin* she remembered about yer bank stickup 20 years ago and it didn't happen at all like what you think.

June didn't sell you out to the sheriff for love or money. She was comin to meet you at this very tree, just like you asked, only the sheriff's boys followed her, and snatched her up before she could call for you.

Then they shot you, Johnny, but I suspect you know that part.

Millie told me that the next day June was found dead in the river. They say she jumped, but her family told everyone it was an accident. Like families do, I s'pose.

But don't you *see*, Johnny, this is the best news! Killin yourself is a sin under the eyes of God. Why, she's probably in hell right now.

Waiting on you, Johnny.

XV

Almost dawn, Johnny, just like the book said.

Feels a little strange to be holdin your bones after talkin to you all this time. I can't even think that they were once under yer skin, 'specially when yer right here in front of me.

Why you so jittery, Johnny? Yer goin to *Hell*, not some church dance. June ain't gonna care what you look like, seein as how yer just as ugly now as you were alive and she fell in love with ya once, didn't she?

Ha, see! *Now* yer not so nervous.

Naw, Johnny, g'on, git. You must be mighty full of yourself to think that Addie May Prichertt can't get on without a nosy ghost lookin over her shoulder. I'll take care of myself just fine, and you do the same.

Though I think, maybe.

The tree won't feel so sad when you're not here. All the sadness is being blown away like dust and fairy lights in the sun.

I'll miss that, I guess.

Goodbye, Johnny Weir.

I reckon we'll see each other again someday.

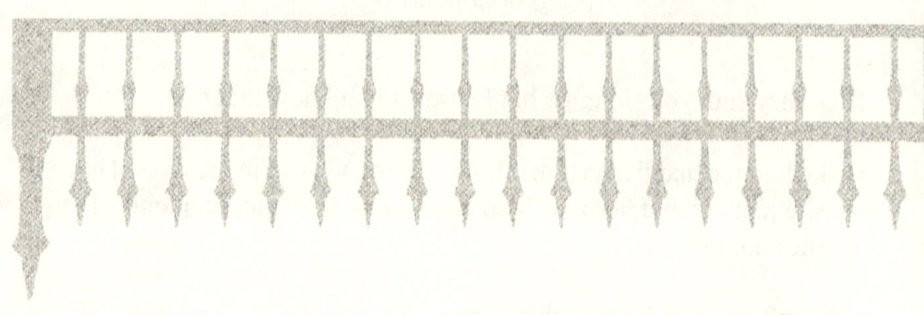

WILD THING

by S.E. ZELLER

Lilibeth wore her best dress the day she met her first. As form fitting as mother would allow her at sixteen, the flared skirt hit just above her knee. Deep blue seersucker fabric crinkled as she moved, much like the oak leaves as they fluttered to the ground around her. She was a sight, she knew, in that dress. Her long legs, scandalously bare above her black and white saddle shoes, were still tanned from the sticky heat of summer.

"What're you doing?" he asked, his resonant drawl drawing an involuntary shiver up her spine. She'd heard him coming, knew it had to be a man. The harsh crunch of the leaves under his feet gave him away, much louder than her own petite feet.

"Gardening," she said, firming the dark soil around the base of the seedling.

"In the forest?"

She nodded at a job well done and stood. He squatted to examine her work as she slid her blade into her pocket and removed her bull hide gloves.

His strong forearms rested on his knees, his wide trunk blocking her view. "Azalea?"

She looked at the top of his head, that straight black hair blowing lightly in the breeze. "Oleander," she said.

He stood and studied her face. Her eyes traced his strong stubbled jaw, his serious hazel eyes.

"Too far north. Might not grow."

"Might not." She lifted her chin with a little shrug.

"Dangerous," he said.

"Beautiful," she countered.

He smiled, slow and deliberate. "You have dirt on your knees." he said, eyes not leaving her face.

"Yes," she said, making no move to brush them off.

He nodded, smile widening. "I'm passing through today, somewhere to be. Want to meet me here Sunday?"

"Can't. Church."

"Saturday then," he said.

She nodded. "Saturday." Lilibeth stood stock still, watching him leave.

He turned around, walking backward, and called out, "What's your name?"

"Lily," she called.

"Hemlock," he said, pointing to himself. He turned and strode away.

Those hazel eyes left her feeling peculiar. Not good, per se, but different. Her curiosity stirred, as if she had suddenly become aware of a new room hidden within her own home.

***

"Carrie," Lilibeth said. The long grass blew in the wind beating against her white ruffled socks. Carrie walked ahead with a new beau. She ignored her seven-year-old sister entirely, clutching to his muscled arm, her careless giggles tinkling back to Lilibeth, irritating her to no end.

"Carrie!" Lilibeth yelled using that singular screeching voice that never failed to cause their mother to eject her from the house.

Carrie continued walking as if Lilibeth didn't exist, but the new beau turned, his dark eyes squinting in the sunlight. Carrie said something to his back, trying to recall his attention, but he was striding toward Lilibeth, broad-backed and upright, as if imagining himself a gallant knight sent to aid the helpless. Carrie's face betrayed her annoyance.

"What is it, little one?" He asked.

Lilibeth cocked her head at him. Not like a dog hearing a whistle, but like an eagle, regarding its prey. She waited for Carrie's reticent step to reach them and pointed a couple feet to Carrie's left. The ground was muddier there that the rest of the field, uneven as if it had recently been turned. Tender shoots of chartreuse stuck out like quills on the back of a porcupine. He glanced at her petite features with uncertainty, but she just continued to point.

As he started toward the muddy ground, Carrie made a tight sound in her throat, reaching weakly for his arm. He pulled up short, and Lilibeth watched the skin on the back of his neck whiten, then flush. He tore off, sprinting away as quickly a gazelle. Lilibeth started to laugh—a little girl's laugh, but deep, deep within her small body. Carrie took one more step toward the spot and screamed at the top of her lungs, fingertips digging into her cheeks.

Lilibeth doubled over, clutching her stomach, tears of mirth running down her face as Carrie screamed bloody murder.

The shallow grave couldn't have been more than two weeks old, and the dirt over the body was recently compacted by rainfall. Poking out of the mud were four human toes.

The big toe had been gnawed off. Only a nub left in its place.

By the time the police came, sent by the now ex-beau, both girls sat on the ground a ways back from the grave. Lilibeth refused to leave until the authorities came, knowing Carrie couldn't leave her. Their mother's repercussions would be far too dire. Carrie clutched goose-pimpled knees to her chin and rocked. She'd turned her back to the decomposing foot, shuddering occasionally. Lilibeth, unflappable, faced it with fascination. Small rivulets of clean skin ran from her eyes, through the dirt, down her chin, evidence of her laughter. Her eyes examined the subtle variations in the colors of decomposition, the bruising around the toenails, the way the earth settled close around the body.

The authorities didn't see. Didn't mark Lilibeth's reaction, notice her enthrallment. Clearly, the child had been terrified and cried herself out. Such a pity that young girls were burdened with such a find.

***

"Lili-Beth. Wash that dirt off your face and put on your town shoes. We're going fabric shopping," her mother said, a smile dimpling her face.

"Bartholomew doesn't like to go to town," Lilibeth said.

"Bartholomew is not invited. You are going. He stays home."

"No. I'm staying with Bartholomew. He doesn't wear shoes. Me neither," Lilibeth said.

"Young lady, it's 'Neither do I.' Look at yourself! You're like a wild thing," her mother said, smoothing her own glossy mane of chestnut hair, her fingers twitching as if they itched to groom her daughter.

Lilibeth shoved a piece of freshly baked dark rye bread into her mouth with one fist, her nails ringed in black soil. Bits of dead grass clung to her dirty blond hair.

"She is a wild thing, mother," Carrie said, her nose flaring as if smelling something foul.

"Enough, Carrie."

"Johnny, why does she have to make up an imaginary friend? No wonder she has no real friends," her mother said.

Her father shook his head behind his book, a frown surfacing on his face.

"Lilibeth, come back here!" Her mother yelled after her, but Lilibeth had already slipped out the backdoor, across the tamed lawn, and into the woods, breathing in the delicious sharp scent of decomposing oak leaves littering the forest floor, and the scent of rain on the wind.

***

Months later, Lilibeth's father found her in the back yard, sitting on the stump of the old maple, her back to him. Her bony shoulders slumped. He wondered when the last time his daughter had bathed.

"Lili-bean," he said, using the pet-name only he called her, "what's the matter, girl?"

The child said nothing, but looked at him, her dark eyes wide and reproachful. He walked toward her, wiping black engine grease off his hands onto a white rag. "Lili, what do you have there?" A note of fear crept into his voice.

Lilibeth cradled a lumpy form in her hands. It was wrapped

in strips of cloth cut crudely from the edge of her brown floral skirt. Before he could make out what it was, he caught the scent of it. Fetid, sickly-sweet decay hit his nose and he gagged. He slowed, approaching with caution.

"Lili?"

And he saw it. The racoon, in the depths of decomposition, had been wrapped like a mummy. Lilibeth looked out of the corner of her eye right past her father.

"Somethin's wrong with Bartholomew's foot."

She stared out toward the forest, and he forced himself to look at the dead thing more closely. The cadaverous racoon's long-nailed toes poked out of the rough bandages on just one paw, four befouled toes, tiny tufts of gray fur hanging from each. One toe was gone, nothing but a nub left in its place.

***

The wood behind Lilibeth's house was afire with fall leaves, the ground a crunchy spate slowly turning to brown. She lay on the forest floor, the edge of her short red skirt fluttering against her browned thighs, watching the wind. She imagined the swirling air currents, the lifts, the downdrafts. She sketched them in her mind, watching leaves fall onto the ground around her. The edges of her glossy crimson lips curved up as she heard the man crunching toward her.

"The forest is beautiful this time of year," he said.

"The forest is always beautiful." Lilibeth raised herself onto her elbows to look at him. She felt a stirring in her belly as her eyes examined him, his hooded dark eyes, the musculature of his thighs through his jeans, his broad shoulders, the set of his jaw. Markedly more mature, more in command, than the fumbling boys who she'd let paw her in the parking lot behind the school, with their scared eyes and inexperienced hands.

"Hemlock is an odd name," she said.

He smiled a lop-sided smile that created a disarming look about his eyes, as if perhaps he couldn't decide whether he was happy or angry to see her. In total it was almost the same look Bartholomew had, years ago, when he fought the other racoon, growling, spitting, attacking, mounting, tumbling about, kicking dust into the air and in her eyes. She'd run that day, the confusion of the animal chaos too much.

"Not odd. Strong," he said.

"Poisonous," she said.

"Resilient," he countered.

"Dangerous," Lilibeth said.

His smile widened, lighting up his eyes. Not a chance she was running this time.

She got to her feet, pulling tight her black cardigan with the small pockets on the front, and shook herself like an animal, leaves flying loose from the back of her dress.

"Would you like to take a walk?"

He nodded. "Anywhere you want." He fell into step with her and offered her his arm. His eyes probed her body. "You still have the forest floor on your skirt and in your hair."

She accepted the arm, feeling his warmth through his light coat. She tightened her grip so that he could feel the curve of her waist, the soft side of her breast.

"And?" She said, not brushing away the forest.

"People may think you've been lying on your back in the forest."

"Let them," she said, and drew him to a nearby tree.

She backed into the trunk, sliding a hand down his neck and pulling him toward her. Leaning in, he kissed her gently on her lips, then harder, with purpose. She pulled him to her by the collar of his jacket and kissed him back, moving her hips against him. He moaned softly, a low, gravely sound. She pulled her mouth away and gave him a smile that didn't reach her eyes. She cocked her head.

"Sit down against the tree," she said, pointing.

He pulled her with him, his hand in her hair, pressing her lips to his. His back slid down the tree, the sound of small pieces of bark crunching and dislodging as he slid to the ground. She straddled him and began to move. His hands ran up her skirt. Lilibeth grabbed them and pushed them onto her taut rear. He ran deft fingers along her, and she moaned. She pushed him back and stood, panting.

He stared at her as his chest heaved, his eyes flashing.

"Come here," he said, and she could see his white teeth bared as he struggled for control.

She lowered her eyelids and stepped out of her white panties, pushing them into her pocket, feeling the bone handle and cold metal inside. He unzipped his pants, and she pulled him on top of her. They moved in tandem, gently at first, then rougher. Her pulling his hair, him growling in his throat, straining into her, her screams as she pulled him in with strong legs as they thrust to climax.

After, they lay on a bed of leaves, and his fingers traced swirls on her skin, like the wind that whirled around them. She rolled over and retrieved her cardigan and slipped it back on, buttoning the front of her dress. She put her hand in the pocket, and he grabbed her wrist.

"Don't put them back on. I'm not done with you yet," Hemlock said. She looked at his hand and smiled into his eyes.

"I'm not done with you either," she said.

His hand was back under her skirt, running strong fingers up and down her body. She shivered deliciously, and pulled her blade from her pocket, concealed in her hand. With her other hand, she stilled his.

"Let me," she said. She kissed his lips, and stroking his exposed chest, she mounted him, rocking quickly on top of him. He raised himself onto his elbows, moving his hips under her. She leaned over and licked one side of his neck hard, and, at his groaned response, brought her other hand up and deftly and deeply sliced his jugular.

She watched the moment of confusion pass over his face, moving from pleasure to pain, rage to panic, and he roared, one hand coming up to his throat, trying to cover the blood rushing from the deep wound, and grabbing her throat roughly with the other. She came powerfully, shuddering deep in her bones, eyes intent on his, watching his final struggle with ultimate satisfaction. His hand started to slack on her neck. She flicked it from her and slipped off him.

Regarding him with a predatory cock of the head, she stepped just far enough away to avoid the pooling blood. When he stilled, she stepped close. She wiped her hand and her blade, sticky with blood, on his jeans. She knelt at his feet. One black wool sock was damp with blood. She slid down the other, running reverent fingers from the ankle down the foot, feeling a tingle of excitement in her belly. She readied her blade for the job.

"Let me see your toes."

THE BEACH

by JULIE HUTCHINGS

Curling my body into a knot wouldn't hide me. If the cliffs hanging overhead didn't darken this sun-drenched nightmare enough, a gaudy beachball-striped umbrella couldn't save me. Not from the cruel heat. Not from the empty blanket beside me.

"Hey Dracula, want a burger? I'll make it bloody." Leering face framed in steam, Davy clacked the tongs together over the sizzling grill.

Clack clack went the coconut crabs on the cliff.

"Never gets old, Davy. No thanks, I'll stick to this," I said, lifting my clear tumbler, careful to stay under the umbrella. I'd dripped red and purple food coloring into my water, for obvious reasons.

"I'm sorry about him," Levi said, putting his hand on my knee—sweet chill—and plopping down beside me.

"No!" I shrieked.

He leaped up and looked behind him, certain he'd see a monstrous crab, something he shouldn't have sat on. And there was something. But only I could see it.

The threadbare beach blanket, faded gray and green with tiny octopuses all over it. *"It's octopi,"* Pearl had always said. Though she was gone, the shadow of the blanket remained on this beach, just out of reach of the creeping black sand.

"I thought I saw something," I lied, and Levi, as kind as always, just smiled and sat on the pristine white sand. One brave gull chose the danger of the smoldering black sand over the mere discomfort of the fiery hot white. He swooped down for a fish left by the tide—now charred from the black beach and the inferno sun, two monsters working together. Within seconds, a coconut crab popped out of its burrow in a burst of steam and snatched the bird with its oven-mitt claw.

I screamed, and Levi took my hand.

"I like what you did with the water," he said in an attempt to distract me, grinning, tapping my tumbler. "It actually looks kinda like blood this time."

Not even a spray of red was left of the gull now.

There hadn't been blood when Pearl disappeared, either.

Locals believed she'd been scared by the crabs, fell from the onyx rock cliffs, and washed out to sea. But those crags didn't invite climbing, and Pearl preferred the beach to adventure. And the crabs weren't predatory. Enormous, yes. But they were out of place, like me. They didn't belong here. Like me.

"You're doing good, babe," Levi murmured, his voice cool and clean against the midnight heat of my mind, threatening to choke and pull me under. He'd been so patient with me since Pearl disappeared, getting me outside, getting me some of that "good ol' D3," as his dad said. I didn't complain that they always brought me to the beach—this beach—because it was their family's home, and they treated me like part of their family. I certainly didn't have one of those anywhere else, especially since losing her.

This beach was the end for me in so many ways. Between the boiling beach and the soothing sea, which both beckoned and terrified me.

"Hey," Levi said softly, tilting my chin between his fingers so I'd stop staring at the empty spot where the octopuses squirmed in the heat-shimmer air, looking back at me. "Don't listen to Davy Jonas," he said loud enough to get a growl from his brother. "He's the devil. But really, you okay?"

"I'm okay," I repeated in little more than a whisper. A thousand times I'd said it over and over in my head, when the gulls screamed, when the blaring music and hiss of the grill drowned me in horrific anxiety which seemed to explode red out of my skin with the slightest hint of sunlight. *I'm okay. I'm okay. I'm okay.* He hadn't known me much before Pearl disappeared, so the dark depths I sunk to afterward were just my personality to him. And yet he still loved me.

He loved me, but he still made me come to this damn beach, even when he knew it was where I lost her.

"Let's go for a swim," he said. Sounded so innocent. So casual. But to get to the ocean, we would have to traverse the black sand.

The water wasn't wild enough to crash menacingly against the cliffs; it was a quietly vicious lapping, a maddening *slap, slap, slap*, humming at the edges of my mind. Levi pulled me to the shore, the ebony sand scorching our feet as we sidestepped crab burrows. "Watch out!" Davy yelled from the shore. "Crab!" I screeched in terror, each of those crabs' claws big enough and powerful enough to snap an ankle.

I was quaking with nerves and blistering by the time we reached the water's edge. At one time, the sand became cooler when approaching the water, a promise of the sloshing sweetness of the salty waves. Not anymore. Approaching the ocean, the sand turned to shockingly hot pitch. Now the holes dug by the coconut crabs spat steam like New York City sewer caps from wet pavement under a rainy night sky.

After one crippling nor'easter at sea, when the dregs of the ocean washed ashore with its broken bottle pieces, its tiny lost treasures, its clumps of seaweed and clamshells, it brought the dark depths with it. And the dark depths never left.

The dark kept coming.

On the first day, the black sand was a wonder to behold. It wasn't tourist season, not yet, so all the locals gathered around the phenomenon in their neon "Plymouth" and "Cape Cod" sweatshirts, clutching their styrofoam coffee cups, their hair blowing in the salt breeze like mermaids on land. We all shivered and toed the mysterious sand that inched up the shore. Where had it come from? Why was it here?

The next week, when the crowd dwindled, the black sand crept ever further up the beach.

And further. Soon, the beach was less white sand, and more black; hot as a fresh Boston blacktop, bursts of steam swelling from its surface in defiance of the cold ocean at its back, hissing, smoking where they met.

The question that haunted me, hunted me:

Had the black sand stolen Pearl—or was the black sand Pearl herself, reaching like demon tentacles to return from the Deep?

Levi and I raced across the burning coal sand, around discarded domes of shells, the *clack clack* giving way to the screaming steam and lapping waves. Toward the hazy mist blanketing the gray ocean.

My seared feet ached for that freezing water and whatever lay beneath it. Whatever would deliver me from this inferno of sun and noise and the constant reminders of who I wasn't and who wasn't there. But as much as I ached for my friend, I didn't want to be part of her ocean. I dreamed of her on that octopus blanket, the crabs scuttling all over her, cracking her bones with their giant claws until she was nothing. Then, from her slivers of skin rose scales. Her hair became seaweed. Her eyes turned to crusty barnacles. Her feet changed, one to a flipper, one to a thin, emaciated tentacle that flopped of its own free will until she slithered and lurched to the sea.

I would strangle her with the damn octopus blanket that she taunted me with day in and day out if she came for me. I loved her, but I would choose this hateful heat over that unnatural oblivion.

"She's so dark all the time," Davy had told Levi, never intending me to hear. *"How can you two stay afloat when she's so deep and dark?"*

Deep and dark.

Levi laughed as he dove into the icy waves, as comfortable there as he was on the torturous shore.

I was never comfortable. Not since the ocean stole Pearl. I'd been cast away here on the beach, and she'd been given the cool, calm depths that I needed.

"Come in," Levi coaxed, his eyes reflecting the water. "The water wants you to come in," he teased.

"I'm afraid," I whispered, to myself, to the ocean, to the world.

But the sun screeched down at me to enter the forgiving water, and no matter what lurked in the sea, I desired the relief more than I feared. The coconut crabs popped up like gophers from their holes, watching to see what I would do. How much I could endure.

Levi splashed in the waves, droplets flurrying around him like enchanted pearls hovering in the air, diving down and popping up playfully with the sun glinting off his ebony hair.

The black sand burned blisters into the soles of my feet. I

wanted to submerge and hear nothing, see nothing but the hidden world under there, solace from the blinding beach.

And I knew the darkness under there would take me too fast.

"Your feet! Hurry!" Levi called to me, fear widening his eyes.

Bubbles of tar formed around my feet, popping through the sizzling steam. *Pop, sizzle, pop.*

My feet boiled, scarlet red and blistering, and I ran for the water even as the black sand reached for me.

Sizzle, pop.

The odor of scorched skin followed me.

Davy's shouts of excitement behind me: "It's moving! The black sand is moving!"

The sea frothed around my feet, blissful, whipped cream cool, making me shudder and melt into the waves. Nothing could be better than this. What could I be afraid of in such silky perfection?

"Come deeper," Levi said in that warm, rich voice of his.

"Come deeper," echoed the sea.

The sky had turned gray, as if a storm was suddenly brewing.

As if a storm had never left.

A shiny, sleek shape cut through the water, a metallic shadow slicing swiftly. It slipped behind Levi, swishing right by him with a flick of its tail.

"Shark," I said, my voice a squeak. I glanced back, the jutting black cliffs stabbing at me. "Shark," I called to the beach, but no one heard me. The rocks saw me, pointed at me, at Levi. Pointed out to the ocean and said, *"Take them."*

"Come on, babe."

"Listen!" I cried. "Levi, a shark!"

I'd forgotten I was in water up to my waist. Frustrated with the way he smiled at me and slicked his dark hair back, glistening in the surf, happy to be alive, I screamed, "Shark!" and slapped the water, aching for him to see that something was *wrong*, that not everything could be solved by a day at the beach. But he dove under. Never listened to me. *Levi Than, why couldn't you just hear me? What if I lose you, too?*

I dove under the frigid water, salt dashing up my nose, and swam as fast as I could, still only nightmare-slow, bubbles streaming after me.

The creature was a moving silhouette, and Levi was so close.

I had to get to him.

Could he see me?

"We see you."

Voices like swooshing fins, soft and gentle, but strong. Strong enough to turn my eyes from straight ahead to where Levi splashed, down through the clear water, so much less murky since the black sand cleansed it.

The deeper I dove, the cooler the caress.

And below, a blanket of smooth ebony stones. I imagined them stroking the soles of my blistered feet, my hair waving in the sea as I walked the silent ocean floor.

Glancing up, I saw two sharks now, swimming in tandem, and Levi treading water between them. He had to know they were there.

"A predator among predators," the voices said below. *"Levi Than,"* they chanted, lulling me. The bubbles trailing behind me flowed slower, but I enjoyed the lack of motion. *"Levi Ahab Than, Levi A. Than, Levi A. Than."*

And more *clack clack clacking*, a sound I'd reserved for the beach and rock cliffs.

The chanting, *"Leviathan, Leviathan." Clack clack clack.*

Lustrous glinting came from below, amongst the stones. Like glitter on velvet.

Pearls. Pearls dotting the black stones like stars in the sky and twice as shiny. Glistening white pearls.

Pearl.

"Priscylla," Pearl's voice called to me.

Clack clack clack.

And when the stones were within reach, and the sharks swarming above were as distant as the white sand, I saw what the pearls really were.

Teeth.

"We see you," the mouths in the stones sang. And their eyes popped open.

Not just stones, then.

Faces.

Gleaming, bared teeth clacking as they sang, *"Leviathan, Leviathan,"* over and over, staring at me unblinking, like all those little octopi. Seaweed as green as Levi's gaze reached from between the faces like tentacles, embracing me.

...the ocean came for me in a blanket of darkness...

"Sssssstay," hissed the chilly voices, welcoming me to forget the hiss of the inky sand above. And one voice in particular.

"Pearl?" I said. Water flooded my mouth, a stark reminder of how treacherous the ocean could be.

"As is the world above."

Whipping my feet frantically, I tried to free myself of the seaweed but only managed to wind myself tighter.

Then a stabbing pain in my feet made me cry out, and once again swallow more salt water, and darkness with it.

I bent in half grasping the seaweed with both hands, and I saw that the pinching, sharp pains were bites.

Floating up like little clams, the rocks bit my feet with piranha teeth.

And teeth gnashed at me from above. Sharks, circling lower. Two…three. No, four.

Like the black sand, the ocean came for me in a blanket of darkness.

I will come for you, *too,* I thought.

"Priscylla," came the melody of voices, Pearl's ringing out loudest. *"Scylla, Scylla, rise up."*

I stopped struggling against the seaweed. I let it join me. The ocean wanted me, and I wanted it just as much.

I will be the storm that never left.

The vibrant green tendrils crawled up my legs, devouring them in their slick frills.

"Scylla…"

I snipped my new appendages free of the rocks below with fresh claws. *Clack, clack.*

I wanted to look up at the sharks, but would not remove my eyes from the smooth faces below, with eyes of every color, their teeth showing soft smiles now. And so I grew new eyes.

Two for above; two for below. So that I could see the delicious depths all at once.

Above, the sharks swam faster, aching to taste me.

I clacked my claws in delight, reaching up with yet more new appendages—endlessly long, thick, death-white tentacles—and plucked the sleek beasts from the shallows, pulling them down to my mouth, which expanded to encompass them, one at a time, in fateful gulps.

"She is Scylla," sang the voices of the deep.

"Priscylla!" rang Levi's voice from above, crystalline clear, looking for the me that I was before.

"She is Scylla," chanted the sea.

Tenderly, I wrapped a tentacle around him, this earthbound sea spirit, and I tugged him down from the surface.

"She is Scylla."

I spread my limbs, my mouth wide. I would hide no longer.

"She is the Leviathan."

NEEDS MUST

by HELEN WHISTBERRY

Eloise is growing impatient again. She wags her finger in my face and mouths those weird whispery sounds that make the hairs along the back of my neck stand to attention.

"Look at the state of her," snickers Jax, and for once, he's right. She's really let herself go. Understandable, given the circumstances, but it is difficult to maintain respect for someone who has allowed themselves to come so completely undone.

Things haven't been the same since that day. How long has it been? Keeping up with the passage of time has never been my strong suit. I tend to live in the moment. If the food bowl is refilled regularly and I'm taken out for my walks, life is good.

But our lovely routine has gone to hell. It's all right for Jax. Once his litterbox got full, he just started relieving himself wherever he wanted. He has no dignity at all, no pride. It was quite the comedown when I had to give in and follow his example. At least I try to keep mine to out of the way corners, but the stench is becoming unbearable.

I miss the outside. The jingle of the keys, the rush to the door. Eloise laughing at my excitement as she tries to attach my leash. Then, the elevator ride down twenty-three floors. How frightened I was of

60

that at first. She had to pick me up and carry me on and off, calling me a 'silly boy' and I was, but puppies are like that. The world is so big and we're so small. I've matured since then, thankfully, else how could I have navigated this unprecedented situation?

We live on a quiet street, away from the noise and congestion just a few blocks over. We've walked that far a few times, but I didn't like the hubbub and let my disapproval be known by howling. I've learned Eloise doesn't like attention, so she quickly hustles me away when I get loud. This has come in handy more than once. It's so important to get to know your owner well so that you can control them. Otherwise, they might run amuck.

Jax uses his claws rather than a howl. He can be sweet as anything when he wants her attention, but the moment he's done, out come those murder spikes. I've warned him about it more than once, but he never listens to me. Now look at the mess we're in. It's entirely his fault, but does he care? Not he. No apology, not one word of regret. Better not to let myself get too worked up about it, though. It's important to preserve energy and practice being calm while we wait.

Eloise could use the practice—she's been on quite the rampage today. The waiting is getting to her. She stalks around the apartment like that caged tiger we saw once on the television. Jax was absurdly fascinated by it and sat with his nose against the screen making those little 'ack, ack' sounds. Eloise fell for it as always, fussing over him like he was some kind of savant for recognizing one of his distant kin. What she sees in that ragged, sprawling animal was always beyond me.

But I digress. As I said, Eloise has been restless, fidgeting all over, waving her hands over the objects she has scattered across every surface, babbling nearly inaudibly and quite incomprehensibly. Jax just raises one lazy eyelid then goes back to snoozing in the sunspot. How he can relax at all in this situation is beyond me. I follow Eloise everywhere. Someone has to keep an eye on her. It's distressing how she continually moans and twirls about like a madwoman. Such a change. Such a sad change.

I try to remember her as she was before. So organized and clean. She was proud once of her long, golden hair. Brushed it nightly and got up early every morning to arrange it in careful coils before leaving for work with a cheerful wave. Now she mopes about in the nightgown she was wearing, her hair hanging down so you can hardly see her lovely face at all. Those shining brown eyes that used to look deep into mine are distracted and dulled.

She's not communicated to anyone but us since it happened. Her phone rang and beeped for a day or two until the battery gave out. There was a knock at the door yesterday. I barked as loud as I could, but I don't know if anyone heard me. The steel doors in this apartment building are thick, and thank goodness the soundproofing is rather good, or at least that's what Eloise has said to me many times when I was raising a rumpus. In our current situation, however, I believe it is not working to our advantage.

Eloise didn't answer the knock at the door, though she did go stand at it, looking quite frantic. She eventually drifted back to the sofa in an attitude of despair that is her most common state these days. I curled up next to her and tried to comfort her as best I could, but I must acknowledge my relative helplessness. It is not a good feeling.

It reminds me of watching her writhing on the bed as the deep scratch Jax had given her on the arm blistered and ran, with me being unable to do anything about it. I puzzled over why she didn't visit the doctor. Maybe it has something to do with this great sickness they talk about on the television. She had gotten very wary of going out more than was absolutely necessary.

Perhaps she thought she could weather the storm by herself. Just a nick from Jax's claws after all, and she's had so many before. The evil thing. I shall never understand the human fascination for cats when dogs are around.

I want it put on the record that the solution to the food crisis was Jax's idea. I was willing to starve when Eloise was no longer able to put our regular snacks out for us. Jax is quite expert at turning on faucets, so shortage of water was never a problem. I believe you can survive quite a while as long as you stay hydrated. I saw that on the television, too.

Jax, however, has no scruples and is a horrible, selfish beast. It wasn't more than a day before he took the first bite. Eloise looked quite horrified and dashed at him, flapping her hands around ineffectually, but with no power to stop him. He paid her no mind, of course. Jax always looks out for number one. I'll never forget the smeary, sticky mess his footprints made as he stalked away after stuffing himself.

I held out as long as I could, but instinct takes over at some point. Easy to judge if you aren't starving to death, I suppose. I thought

Eloise would be sadly disappointed in me, but she just nodded her head gently when she caught my eye, as though to say, while she naturally could not quite approve, she understood. Needs must, after all.

Ah, another knock at the door! I hope they don't give up this time. Our food is turning sour and rancid, and poor Eloise looks more and more distressed every time Jax or I jump up on the bed for another meal. I suppose we'll be taken away from here when we're finally discovered.

I wonder if Eloise will linger behind. She's lived in this apartment for twenty years. She may prefer to remain in familiar surroundings. If another cat or dog moves in, I hope they will treat her kindly. The humans will ignore her, I'm sure, just as they mostly did while she was living. Such a thoughtful, loving owner, though. I hope my next will be as good.

WHAT WE SOW

by TAYLOR JORDAN PITTS

On the day marked in red, Bea and Rose become orphans.

"What," Rose says, the end of her sleeve in her mouth, all damp with spit and tears. It's one of the few words she ever says. It could mean anything to anyone.

Bea looks at the place just past her pa's shoulder. They always used to look so big before, his shoulders. Now they're small and still against the floor where he sat himself down with a bottle of poison in the early hours of the morning. He'd spoken to Bea about it matter-of-factly, which she had appreciated. They didn't need to talk about why he planned to do it—they both knew why. All the gaping cupboards and their cobwebs knew why.

Bea's gaze drifts to the sliding door that leads outside, where the soil is cracked and dry, and brittle brambles line the communal courtyard. Where orphaned stumps bleached white from the sun sit where trees once stretched their branches toward the sky. Where the reapers wait and watch. And where once a year, they come to take their tithe.

Still, even though she knows why, even though every single part of her knows *why*, Bea aches in her chest. In the place Pa told her she might, where her ribs meet her sternum. She clenches her fists.

Tomorrow, Bee, he'd said to her, mispronouncing her name like he always had. Made her promise. She stares at the date on the calendar, the red *O* scrawled haphazardly around it. First day of harvest. Reaping Day.

Time to pay the tithe.

It's a good thing, she reminds herself. They'll get money for their offering, and then Rose won't starve. Bea looks at her little sister now—far too little. The handed-down sweater is twice as big on Rose as it was on Bea when she was eleven.

The reapers will come and take their pa away and pay them so they can buy food. But doubt gnaws at the hollow of Bea's stomach. How much food will their pa's body be able to buy? How many years will they be able to stretch their earnings at the price of his life? Bea swallows, letting herself think the thought she's been avoiding since this plan took root.

How much longer before the cupboards empty again, and Bea goes looking for her own poison?

The clock on the wall says it's still early in the day. The reapers make their call at sundown. Bea chews her bottom lip, trying to ignore her sister's big, watery eyes. She's waiting for Bea to make a decision. For her to act. And Bea *does* have an idea, but it's crazy. The reapers expect death on the harvest. Bea suspects her pa and the other parents in the village had made some sort of pact, come to some agreement about the order in which each of them would die long ago. Part of her thinks Pa had known how and when he would die since the day she was born. The reapers *never* leave without a tithe.

Rose decides the one sleeve is too damp and switches to the other. A sharp pang twists inside Bea. She does not blame their pa for doing what he did. She is not angry with him. But she knows—in the place where her ribs meet her sternum—that she can never do that to Rose.

She cups her fear like precious rainwater and lets it go. "We bury him."

***

It takes a long time to drag the body out of the house and into the courtyard. By the time her pa is faceup on the stone walk, Bea's shirt is soaked with sweat. She finds one of his old checkered shirts and drapes it over his face so maybe Rose will stop staring, wound

Where once a year, the reapers come to take their tithe.

tight, like he's going to jump back to life any minute.

Together, they strike the hard, pitiful dirt of the long-dead garden with rusty shovels they found in the closet. Bea has hazy memories of Pa tilling earth in the quiet dark of dawn, where no one could see. Except Bea, who would watch him work from her bedroom window. But that was years and years ago. She's not even sure if it was real or just a dream.

It hasn't rained in months, and the soil is like a stubborn animal, defying the press of their shovels. After an hour of chipping away at the top layer of dirt, dread coils in Bea's gut. At this rate, they won't bury their pa by nightfall. Judging by the sun, it's already well past noon.

Rose drops her shovel and goes inside. Bea slumps against a dilapidated bench, staring unseeing at its grotesque carved legs. A prickling feeling she can't place raises the hairs on the back of her neck, and she looks around the courtyard. The windows punched into the brick facades of the surrounding houses are dark, but Bea swears she sees movement in one of them, a shadow cutting through shadows. But the longer she looks, the more she doubts her own eyes.

When Rose returns, she has a jug of water in her arms. The dread that had made a home inside Bea—for good, it seems—multiplies. They never waste water. But is this a waste, when it's for Pa? He would have chided them and called them silly, squandering perfectly good water on worm food. But Pa isn't here, and Bea bets even the worms are thirsty too.

She cracks the jug's lid and drenches the earth. Muddy water splashes onto her bare knees. When they dig again, the soil is pliant and obedient, shifting with their shovels like it's been waiting for them—for this day. It piles up in eager clumps as the sun draws a determined path across the sky.

Just before twilight, they pull Pa into the shallow grave. Lightning bugs wink as they scrape wet earth over cold flesh. Even when it's done, Bea still has that creeping feeling, like walking through a spiderweb. At every small snap of a twig, her head shoots up, eyes wide. Lamps have been lit in some of the houses, and now it's unmistakable, what that feeling is.

They're being watched.

Bea stares at the silhouettes hovering behind curtains and realizes, for the first time, that they've never met their neighbors. She never thought about it before—privacy is like water and food, a luxury to be coveted—but now, it seems strange that she's lived steps away from these people her whole life and doesn't know their names. Do they know hers? Pa's?

She picks up the shovels and the empty jug and leads Rose back inside. The house feels bigger than it ever has. Together they wash up, and then Bea heats a can of beans on the gas stove. Night descends in full by the time they finish eating, and the courtyard is shrouded, the wet patch of earth impossible to make out in the dark, even with the gentle light spilling in from the surrounding houses.

They wait all evening, curled up beside one another in a nest of blankets. But the reapers do not come.

They do not come the next day, or the next.

***

Their canned goods only last through December. Bea gives Rose the bigger portions and starts to savor the taste of her own saliva. In the days between one year and the next, days that have festive little drawings on the calendar—scribbled ghosts of Pa—they get lucky. A rabbit gets its foot caught in a snatch of ice right over their pa's grave. It's a scrawny thing, but so are Bea and Rose, and somehow, they make it last.

In the spring, the house feels a little less empty, a little less hollowed-out. One morning, Rose comes running in from the court-yard, wild hair tangled around her neck, something small clutched in her hands. "What!"

"What—" Bea echoes, taking the stem between her fingers. The bud is just barely formed, a sad, runtish thing, soft yellow folded under cool green. She lifts it to her nose and inhales the scent of earth, of life.

They spare some water from the jug for the soil every few days after that. The winter had been hard in many ways, but it had snowed enough to store up water to last them through the dry season. Over the months, the shriveled bud that Rose had pulled multiplies into a sprawling garden. Bea wonders if their neighbors will come outside to enjoy the new life the way she and Rose do—if they will come sit on the cracked benches or the bleached-white stumps, sharing stories of their secret lives under the hot sun. But Bea never sees more than the suggestion of people through window glass. By autumn, even the gargoyles are swallowed up in greenery, and unidentifiable fruits fall from vines into the dirt, where they rot if Bea and Rose aren't diligent about harvesting them. Instead of the passing of days, Bea marks the loss of them as the red circle on the calendar draws nearer.

She wonders who will pay the tithe. Will the reapers demand extra, since there was none last year? She carries flecks of guilt with her always, like dirt under her fingernails she can't scrub out.

On Reaping Day, Bea and Rose pass hours in their garden. That's how Bea thinks of it now—their own special place, close to Pa. Safe. She runs her hand over new leaves that have sprouted. Rose nibbles on a piece of fruit, red juice dripping down her chin and soaking into the greedy earth at her knees.

Funny, Bea thinks, that nothing used to grow here. Just last year, the courtyard was a wasted scrap of useless land. She watches Rose eat her fruit, and suddenly she gets that creeping sensation again, the one she hasn't felt in a long time. There's something unseemly about the juice on her sister's chin, something a little grotesque. The sun is almost gone, now, and a chill sweeps through the courtyard, stirring the leaves. Bea shivers.

Where are the reapers? she wonders. And who will pay their tithe?

There are no lightning bugs out. No lights in the windows, no shifting curtains. But there is that feeling.

When Bea hears the snapping of twigs, something inside her cracks too—the place where rib meets sternum. Figures dressed in black line the courtyard. The barest suggestion of people, they stand, and they watch.

Bea holds her breath. Rose hasn't seen them yet, at least. Her hands are full of the red, red fruit, and Bea realizes what had bothered her before. Why the soil of the courtyard had been barren for so long. It had been waiting, *dying*, until a tithe was paid—not to the reapers, but to the earth.

Snap. Crack.

As they approach in the dark, Bea grabs her sister's slick hand. The fruit falls to the ground between them, where it stays. And rots.

ALWAYS AN AFTER

by A.P. HOWELL

She is awake.
She is awake, in darkness.
She is awake, in darkness, hearing a noise.
She is awake, in darkness, hearing a different noise.
(More than one noise is possible. Not all things happen at once.)
Dark is replaced by light.
(Light and dark both exist, but do not happen at once.)
There is a face. The eyes are open, then briefly close. This happens more than once.
(Faces exist. There are many, and they have many expressions. Not all faces, not all expressions, happen at once.)
There is a crackling noise. She sees blue and then darkness.
(There are many colors. Not all colors are visible at once.)
She is awake, in darkness.
("At once" is about time. Time is also with her.)

***

One of the noises is more than one noise: a click and a creak.

(Things that happen together are not always the same thing. They may be related. Things can be related.)

One of the noises is a crackle. Plastic can crackle and plastic can be blue. She thinks the crackle is plastic.

(Things can have more than one attribute.)

Faces are things that can be remembered. She remembers the face that appears. She does not remember seeing the face before it began appearing like this.

("Before" is part of time. Not everything is "now.")

***

The click and creak happen, and then the crackle. The face appears.

The face is part of a body. She thinks it is a woman.

(Faces—bodies—people have attributes.)

Behind the face is something metal. Behind that is gray. It makes a soft sound in imitation of the crackle. She thinks it is also plastic.

(Things can have similar attributes but not be the same thing.)

The woman's hands are gloved. The woman moves the blue plastic and it is dark.

(People and things can have attributes. She has attributes.)

***

There is a soft crackle. She remembers the noise. It has happened before.

Then there is a click and a creak. There is a louder crackle, and then there is light.

She recognizes the woman who moves the plastic away from her face. The woman who stands in front of another sheet of plastic.

The thing the woman ducks under, the metal, is part of a car.

(She remembers what cars are, from sometime before now.)

If she is looking up at that, it means that she is lying in the trunk of a car.

(People are not supposed to lie in car trunks, wrapped in plastic. She remembers that from before.)

***

She is not moving now. She used to move.

She tries to move now, in the darkness.

She cannot. She does not think it is because she is wrapped in plastic.

***

Emotions are things she remembers. Things from before.

She suspects that before, she would have felt fear, had she been in this situation.

(It is a complicated thought, involving hypotheticals and twisted verb tenses.)

She is not afraid. She is not concerned about the ways in which her now might change or the ways in which before was different. At most, she is faintly curious about after.

(Curiosity is an emotion.)

There is always an after. She simply needs to wait.

***

The woman returns. She opens the trunk and unwraps the tarp. She takes notes. She raises a camera to take a picture. Then she rewraps the plastic and closes the trunk of the car.

The woman who opens the car trunk has a name. She wonders what it is.

She wonders what her own name is. She is certain she had one before, and sees no reason why it should not be the same now, and after.

(She thinks this in the dark. She exists even when the other woman is not looking at her.)

She thinks her name was Claire.

Her name is Claire.

***

Claire knows she has seen many other people, before. They had names.

She tries to remember faces. She can remember some.

She examines her emotions. Some faces bring pleasure, some

sadness, some a mix of both.

One face elicits many emotions, but they are all mixed with affection. Love. It is a man's face, or sometimes a boy's face; but it is always the face of the same person.

(People's faces can change, but who they are does not change.)

Matthew. His name is Matthew. Or Matt. Mostly Matt.

***

There are more senses than sight and sound, she remembers. Before, she could also smell and taste and feel. She wonders why she cannot do so now. Then she tries to imagine what she might smell and taste and feel now.

(She remembers remembering that people are not supposed to lie in car trunks wrapped in plastic.)

The thought fills her with unease and her mind refuses to grasp hold of the question.

***

The woman returns. Claire expects the recurring stimuli. She enjoys it.

The woman makes her notes and takes her photograph. She frowns and reaches somewhere behind Claire's head, withdrawing a rectangular object smaller than an index card. It is mostly putty-colored, with some pink. The woman shakes the object and taps at it and says "Dammit."

She is unhappy. All those things mean she is unhappy.

"I'm sorry," Claire says.

The woman sighs and begins to rewrap her.

***

There are other noises in the dark. Outside the car trunk, she can hear animals and thunder. Raindrops strike the car.

(This means the outside plastic has been moved, otherwise the raindrops would make a different sound.)

There are noises inside the car trunk as well. Insect noises.

***

"Hello," Claire says when the woman opens the trunk and begins to remove the plastic.

"Hello," the woman replies.

(Did she hear? That seems unlikely. But none of this seems particularly likely.)

***

"Before" takes on a different shape and texture. Before-now has become before-the-trunk.

(She knows what this means but does not think too hard about it. There are others things that can be the focus of her curiosity, however, and she is tender toward her sluggish emotions. There will be time.)

Before-the-trunk, she remembers stepping on a bee while barefoot. It was painful and she cried, first because of the pain and then because of the dead bee. She hadn't meant to hurt it; she just hadn't seen it. Matt was there. He made fun of her wails until he realized she was really hurt, and then he immediately ran to get an ice pack and tell their parents.

(It is a complicated memory, a tangle of emotions she picks at for a long time.)

She remembers a funeral, dressed in black beside Matt and their father, the three of them in shock. She remembers a word: aneurysm. It meant no chance to say goodbye.

(This is not a complicated memory. It is large and layered but all the layers involve grief.)

She remembers another funeral, once again dressed in black beside Matt. This time, there is more exhaustion than shock. She remembers trips to the hospital, discharges, readmissions. Heart disease had meant many chances to say goodbye, all of which felt premature.

(This is a more complicated memory. It involves not only grief, but also relief and guilt and selfish sadness.)

She remembers sitting with Matt after the sympathetic visitors had returned to their own homes, sandwiches and crudité eaten, memories shared. They opened the liquor cabinet they had never dared raid as teenagers, and drank a miserable toast to their status as adult orphans.

(She knows why she thinks so much of funerals.)

***

"Hello," Claire says when the woman opens the trunk.

"Good morning," she responds absently.

(It is a response, Claire is certain, because the woman has never greeted her before.)

The woman checks near her head and Claire asks "Is it working today?"

A shake of the head and an annoyed frown count as an answer, perhaps. The woman turns to her visual examination, her notes and her camera.

"Goodbye," Claire says as she is rewrapped.

"Later," the woman says, and slams the trunk shut.

***

It makes no sense that she can speak but cannot move. Speaking requires movement: lips, jaw, tongue, lungs; muscles and connective tissue and organs working in concert.

(It makes no sense that she can speak.)

So if she can speak, it logically follows that she can move. She tries her fingers first, then her toes. She cannot feel the plastic, but she has never been able to feel the plastic. She thinks she can feel her fingers flex.

Before, there was a piano. She did not play often, but did play sometimes. Now, she flexes her fingers in a remembered pattern, playing silent music on a piano that does not exist.

***

"Hello," she says.

"Good afternoon," the woman replies.

After unwrapping, Claire sits up. It is a strange change of perspective, after so long spent in the car trunk.

(Why should this change her field of vision? Surely her eyes are no longer responsible for what she sees.)

The woman does not appear to notice, bending past Claire to examine what lies in the trunk. Claire swings her legs up and exits the trunk.

(This is not possible without touching the woman. But she does not react and Claire's consciousness elides these moments.)

She waits until after the wrapping and the trunk closure. The woman lifts the gray plastic and begins to roll it up, fixing it in place on top of the car.

"Goodbye," Claire says as the woman turns away and walks away.

Claire looks down at the car, now that it feels safe to do so. It is old, blocky, with scratches and dents in the silver paint. A Pontiac Bonneville, she sees, while making a circuit of the vehicle. One headlight is missing, a gaping hole in crumpled metal; one tire is flat and another is very flat. The seats are empty and torn. She searches her memory, but does not think she has ever seen this car before.

(She remembers riding in a car, nauseous and exhausted, with Matt at the wheel. She drove cars, too, but the memory of rides when she could not is particularly strong.)

The car is in the middle of the woods, not at all the sort of place where cars are usually found. The passage of the car, and another vehicle with a wider track (a tow truck?), have left ruts in the earth.

Claire looks around at the wider world. Hickories rise and form a partial canopy over the car. Sunlight dapples the ground. The wood is pleasant, a place she could imagine hiking.

(She used to hike, she remembers. Before…and before.)

She follows the woman through the woods until they come to a second car. It is blue, and like Claire's it is old and dented and has a plastic tarp attached to the roof. The woman has unrolled it over herself and the trunk.

Claire looks away. She already knows what is happening there. Watching will not sate any curiosity.

Walking back to her car, a splash of color catches her attention. Downhill, yellow crime scene tape winds around trees, delineating a square patch of earth.

(She remembers watching police dramas and murder mysteries. The yellow tape evokes scenes shot at night, with red and blue flashing lights illuminating investigators and throngs of curious observers. The yellow tape evokes a sense of urgency not at all evident in the woods.)

Within the square, there are bodies.

Two are dressed in sweatpants and t-shirts. The arm of one is extended beyond the border of the tape. A bird worries at the head of the other. Two more bodies are wrapped in plastic tarps.

(She wonders if the tarps were purchased at the same time, from the same place, as her own. Then she allows the thought to slide away.)

Claire turns away and walks back up the hill. She finds the Pontiac and sits beside her car.

***

Her arms look fat. She studies them for a time, and then realizes that her arms look the way they did for years. It was only later that they grew thin, bones prominent and skin punctured by needles. They simply look strange because she has forgotten what her arms looked like when she was healthy.

(Having healthy looking arms now, she decides, is a funny thought. She had a sense of humor before, and perhaps it is returning.)

She remembers the drip of chemicals, scheduling appointments, charting good days and bad days. Poisoning herself in the hopes that the cancer would die first.

"Are you sorry?" she remembers Matt asking, not questioning her reaction to the diagnosis but to her choice to treat it.

"No," she had said then, and it was half a lie at that moment. She remembered being so very, very exhausted that day.

(It was not the last day. Claire did not think she could remember the last day—which had, apparently, not actually been her last day of consciousness—but it was close.)

She remembered all the days when she had felt determined or angry or sad for Matt, who was going to lose what remained of his family, and for herself, who was going to lose decades of life. "Fuck cancer."

"Fuck cancer."

"And who knows? Maybe they'll learn something." Data points from her treatment could help improve medical outcomes for others. She lifted her glass. "I dedicate my body to science."

"To science," Matt had said, tears in his eyes. There had so often been tears in his eyes, though he only rarely cried in her presence. She remembered feeling gratitude for both facts.

(She feels something like gratitude now, that she knew him

for her entire life and has overwhelmingly warm feelings for him.)

*****

Claire remembers that the woods are supposed to be frightening at night, even when the woods in question are not also a graveyard, but she finds the place calming. The stars are out, visible through the canopy, and the moon limes the leaves with silver. Small animals go about the business of survival. Their bodies rustle in the underbrush, owls hoot and occasionally descend upon their prey. She knows that somewhere, still beyond her hearing, bats hunt insects.

(Insects, too, are busy. She does not think too carefully about this.)

*****

"I think you can hear me," Claire says to the woman, who pauses for a moment in her work. She has unrolled the tarp on the roof of the blue car, clearly ready to collect her data. "Can you hear anyone else?"

The woman says nothing. Claire wanders away to look at the exposed bodies. She did not do so yesterday—it felt too voyeuristic—but now curiosity has gotten the better of her.

The bodies are well into the decomposition process. The skin has darkened, the eyes are missing, and insects cluster near the mouth and nose and ears. It is, she reflects, quite a disgusting sight, and there is something viscerally disturbing about the rotting faces in particular. But her emotional reaction is somewhat muted. These people were alive, now they are not, and so of course their bodies are consumed.

(She remembers watching *The Lion King* with Matt, singing along about the circle of life.)

She wonders if the people are well and truly gone, or if she simply cannot perceive them. Contemplating these questions does not disturb her, but merely engages her curiosity.

Claire thinks she was like this before, too. Perhaps it is easier to feel this way now. Visceral reactions are surely more difficult when one lacks viscera.

(This too is a funny thought. She wishes she could share it with Matt.)

***

Claire wanders farther into the woods. She is beginning to think of them as her woods.

She makes her way down hills and back up again, still moving as she would have before. She seeks clear paths between the trees, avoiding thick underbrush and ducking under branches. Claire observes the wildlife, enjoys the birdsong and hum of insects.

There are more bodies. Some lie naked; others are dressed; some are wrapped in plastic. A few lie inside metal cages, protected from the attentions of larger animals. There are also burial sites, some shallow and others noticeable only because of recently disturbed dirt. She comes upon a barrel, closed against the elements, and supposes a body is folded inside.

She also finds another car as decrepit as her Pontiac. This one has been placed under full sunlight. Claire is not surprised to see it, and finds herself concerned by the small sample size of the woman's experiment.

(She has warm thoughts for the woman. This, even more than a selfish desire to be of use, motivates her concern. Claire wants the woman's experiment to be a success.)

***

By sunrise, she has settled on the ground near the parking lot, criss-cross applesauce. At some point it occurs to her to glance downward. She recognizes the t-shirt and sweatpants as her favorite loungewear, and smiles at the chocolate stain on the front of the shirt.

(She will never taste chocolate again. Maybe that should upset her, but instead she is filled with pleasure from the memory of chocolate.)

A car approaches and parks in a space near the fence. The woman emerges, then spends some time gathering up her equipment before entering the woods.

"Good morning," Claire says.

The woman's stride changes slightly, her body reacting before her mind can overrule it. She says nothing, but Claire does not mind.

"I think you can hear me," Claire says. "You don't have to be embarrassed. There's no one else here."

She follows the woman to the gray car—her car—and watches as she unrolls the tarp on the roof. Claire steps next to her, sharing the space under the plastic.

(There may not be enough space. The plastic may pass through her. Later, perhaps, she will think about that and conduct experiments of her own.)

Claire holds an imagined breath as the woman unlocks the trunk. She is not entirely sure she wants to watch, but feels it is important that she do so.

The woman makes notes—judging by her scowl, the data logger is still malfunctioning—and then begins to unwrap the body in the trunk.

The skin is blotched, sickly and darker than Claire remembers. The texture is entirely wrong, with a soapy sheen. In some places, it clings to bone; in others the bone is exposed. Maggots writhe in the tarp.

Claire recognizes the t-shirt and sweatpants. She stares longer at the face. The changes wrought by decomposition make it nearly unrecognizable. But it is a face Claire saw every day in the mirror. She traced its transformation from childhood to adolescence to adulthood, from health to terminal sickness.

She has always been able to recognize her own face.

The woman takes her photographs and makes a few more notes, then rewraps the body. Claire releases an imagined breath.

Nothing has changed, nothing has happened, except she did something important.

(She has chosen her own after, within this larger after since her death.)

She is not certain what will happen next, but she is certain that there will be a next. That is the way time works. That is the way the world works. Claire feels no fear, only curiosity, because that is the way she works.

There is always an after.

GHOST LIGHT
or, TO SWELL SO HIGH THAT HE MAY DROWN HER IN HIM

by ELOU CARROLL

'Erik is not truly dead. He lives on within the souls of those who choose to listen to the music of the night.'
—Gaston Leroux, *The Phantom of the Opera*

'I looked upon the sea, it was to be my grave.'
—Mary Shelley, *Frankenstein; or, The Modern Prometheus*

Beneath the wheeze of the water wheel and the rush of the waves, G. Leroux's Museum of Theatrics sings into the gloaming. Its song is carried so far across the great grey meadow that the saltlarks scream of ghosts in the water. Below, the saltlarks say, London is whispering. Below, they say, if you press your face down to the tide, you can see the dome of St. Paul's brushed green with algae, and the eyes of God leering up.

As Madrigal moors her dinghy, she does not look down. It is bad luck to look upon the drowned world. Instead, she looks up. A haphazardly scrawled poster has been affixed to the side of the museum since the interview; the original headline crossed out. *Come One, Come All! New Interactive Exhibit Coming Soon*, it says now. ~~*Come and See! Feast Your Eyes on the Dancer from the Deep!*~~ *The Star of the Show: Theatreland in Miniature!* is scribbled in small, uneven letters underneath.

"Out with the old, in with the new, I say," calls the man who is not G. Leroux. The name taken from the cover of a book but rightly, his name is Portico Junk. "You must be our *artiste*. Come to make sure the show goes on!"

Madrigal winces at the pronunciation. "Artist, yes."

When she was a girl and Gramma was done with the fire, Madrigal took the burnt driftwood pieces in her hands and scrawled across the homeraft—since then, she and Gramma have traded art for fish hooks, the little boat on which she sails, and news from across the grey. It was from a passing saltlark that Madrigal heard of G. Leroux's Museum of Theatrics.

Madrigal collects her trunk of brushes, palettes, and paints from the bottom of the boat. She hefts her pack onto her shoulder, scrolls of thick, greenish paper spilling out of the top.

"Now, where d'you get a thing like that?" Portico casts a covetous eye on the pages. "That's a rare thing."

"We make the pulp from seaweed."

"Excellent," he says. "Most excellent. Ingenuity will get you far, my girl."

***

The museum looks larger now that she is standing beneath it, as if it has grown up out of the surf. Though it is fashioned after the theatres from old world photographs, it is built entirely from scrap. No longer a place for performance, it is filled with things rescued from the West End under the waves, and further. As Madrigal enters, the museum lets out a hush like it might be breathing—tasting the salt on her skin and deciding when to bite.

Portico trots into the foyer, pointing at posters and long-ago merchandise procured, he says, from the original Royal Opera House by his *own* fair hand. A case of sea-mottled photographs hangs along one wall. Long-dead faces smile out with exaggerated expressions.

Portico leads her past every exhibit, poring over each of his wonders. "Look," he says. "Look and see."

A ballet dancer is mounted on a plinth in the centre of what would have been the principal dressing room, framed with light bulbs—the electricity stutters intermittently.

She looks as if she has been lifted from the seabed—the Dancer from the Deep, the poster had said. Her skin is grey, rough, hair dark and pressed with pearls and seaweed. She is wrapped in a tangle of fishing nets, as if she'd been caught and dragged to land, an attempted escape dishevelling the scales on her cheeks.

Madrigal thinks of the photographs in the foyer. In one, the principal dancer with a group, tucked in the back, unsmiling; another, a close up of her face, lips slightly parted, eyes pleading. The dancer is dying in the final image—arms cast out at her sides, she is held up by a man swathed in black. Her back is arched so that she is almost folded back on herself. Her face scrunched in agony. They could be the same, the girl in the photographs and the girl on the plinth.

Madrigal stares into the eyes of this drowned dancer, so bright they could be real, and shivers. When she leans in close to inspect the costume's fine stitching, nails, sharp and hard like bone, catch in Madrigal's salt-stiff curls.

The artist stills, breath caught like a stopped clock, pulse thrumming staccato beneath her skin. Madrigal squeezes the strap on her bag, knuckle-white, and gapes at the dancer's mould-encrusted ballet slippers.

Don't look up don't look—

A laugh peals through the museum, light as a bell but cracked underneath. Madrigal reels back, a tuft of red tearing from her scalp. Sucking in a shaky breath, she raises her head with her eyes closed. When finally the idea of not-seeing is worse than the thought of what she *might* see, her eyes open. The curl is clutched between the dancer's fingers and a smile spreads sharp-toothed across her face.

"The look on you," the dancer cackles. "You've had quite the fright, best just go home."

"Allegra." Stern-faced, Portico shakes his head. A glance passes between them—Portico chin raised, and the dancer sour, as if she's holding something rotten beneath her tongue. He inclines his head, and the dancer relents.

"I think this belongs to you," says Allegra, now without humour.

e looks as if she has been lifted from the seabed—the Dancer from the Deep.

She holds out the ripped curl and dumbly, Madrigal takes it—holds it close against her chest as if it might noose her racing heart.

Portico stifles a cough, presses it into his beard with his palm, eyebrows drawn down and dark. "Allegra, if you please. You never know when a visitor might approach—we must protect the mystery, the magic, the beauty that is *theatre*."

Allegra climbs gracefully back onto the plinth and resumes her pose. She stares—cold—at Madrigal and the girl shrinks back. If she looks closely at the dancer's knees, she can see the rough texture of paint, the slight wobble in the line of the ball joints. Not a doll at all.

"Come, come," says Portico. He skitters down corridors bright once more, flitting between artefacts—"Imagine! Just imagine!"—until they reach backstage. If it were a real theatre preparing for a show, and not the ghost of one held tight, it would be teeming with activity. Performers stretching and singing their vocal cords into submission. Wiggies and dressers at work. A hurried director calling last-minute instructions, the rustling chatter of an audience scratching at his nerves.

As it is, the area is in disarray. Photographs are strewn hither and thither, and materials are piled haphazardly along the back wall. Near its base, mould creeps eating the scrap with rotted teeth.

"And this," he says, "is your kingdom. Here, you will create a world in miniature—do make yourself at home."

Madrigal pores through the photographs—there are so many of them, so many scenes beyond her water-logged comprehension. She tries to imagine a world that does not rock and roil at the whim of the waves, where the ground is still and there are miles and miles without a port in sight. Where there isn't a drowned world at all.

"Where did you get—" When Madrigal turns, Portico is gone and the museum is draped in growing shadows—is it that late already?

She is barred from the stage by a thick curtain, red and mottled, with ragged edges and holes where a small light slips through. Madrigal creeps past the fabric—the house lights are low and the only real illumination comes from an old, flickering bulb on a rickety frame sitting centre stage.

"What *is* that?" she mutters, jumping at the soft sound of a footstep.

"That's the Ghost Light." Allegra materialises from the wings. The light does not reach the pits of her eye sockets, but her painted irises sparkle in the dim. "To ward off the dead when the house lights are out."

***

A draft glides through the museum, and on it rides the crackling notes of an aria played through the museum's salt-salvaged speakers. The voice of some long-dead ingenue calling out.

Madrigal has paint in her hair and a song on her tongue; she knows the museum's recordings as she knows the lines on her palms. They are not as welcoming as Portico intended. Instead, they are far away—something is missing. Lost. Just when Madrigal thinks she's caught it, it slips between her fingers. In all of her to-ing and fro-ing between the museum and the homeraft, where there is always a pot of Gramma's fish stew on the boil and a laugh in her belly, she has yet to see another soul sailing to the museum.

"A dry spell," said Portico when she asked. "That's all. When you're finished, you'll see. Your miniatures will be the talk of the salt. Just wait."

On the hobbled work bench in front, three exteriors are drying, pale as crushed pearls. The facades of theatres, half from photographs, half from inside Madrigal's chest. Tiny gargoyles peer out from one roof, their lurid faces snarling. Another has windows painted so warm that there might be lights on inside. The third, the tallest, is adorned with a golden arabesque panel, like the hidden treasure of a story Gramma told her as a fuzzy-headed child with charcoal on her fingers and smudges on her cheeks.

When the music changes, G. Leroux's Museum of Theatrics is silent but for the whir of the water wheel and the hum of the generators it powers. Briefly, there is the electric fizz of dipping lights.

And beneath all of that is the soft *swish* of Madrigal's brush. She paints a stage with all of its trappings. Figures in still poses, on tracks that can be pushed and pulled to give the illusion of performance. With a fine brush, she paints a pair of deep red lips—the owner of which is falling into a faint, caught, she supposes, by the dashing lead. Or not. Madrigal has yet to decide. With the tiny performers in hand, the artist wonders if this might be what it is to be God. A tired chuckle escapes her lips, and she catches it in her hands. Madrigal casts a nervous glance over her shoulder—but no one is there to see.

She brushes a palm across her forehead, smearing her face with paint. The air is stuffy despite the deepening cold.

The speakers click back to life. This time, a rich, unfamiliar bass sings forth. His voice so deep Madrigal can feel it in her chest—in her bones. When she directs her hand back to its task, it trembles.

Oh, here you are, a madrigal singing me to sleep—

She stills. Her heart drums in her ears. There is no music save his voice and the whisper of the waves—so intimate, he could be behind her with his hand across her throat. Then, his voice swells so loud, she might drown in it.

Oh, when I gaze upon your face, I'll raze us to the deep.

She wets her lips and swallows. The voice hums long and low.

Madrigal presses a hand to her stomach—the note is there, anchored deep like ballast. She shakes her head—air, she needs air.

Outside, the music is louder, but the song has changed. Choral, it sings of weeping.

And drowning.

Madrigal shakes until the ends of her fingers turn blue.

***

"Where did you find the new music?" Madrigal leans into the box office where Portico Junk sorts through boxes, throwing things aside with a sneer and a shake of his head.

Portico stills. He looks up at the artist, opens his mouth only to close it again. He shakes himself then, and stretches a smile across his lips though it does not reach his eyes. "I've no new music, poppet. Just the same as I've always had. Records are difficult to come by, now-a-days. Especially quality. I can't have just anything, my pet."

"But I thought…" She presses her mouth into a thin line.

"Hm?" Portico is no longer listening, his attention caught by wet feathers. Something long and damp and coiled at the bottom of the box. It looks like a bedraggled seabird, clubbed and come to shore. He lifts it carefully, like a babe—"Aha!"—and wraps it cold about his neck. "Brilliant."

Allegra watches them from down the hall, her paint smudged and cracking. When Madrigal raises a hand in greeting, the dancer turns away.

She's not sure when she decides to follow, but soon Madrigal climbs the spine of the museum, clambering up slim staircases and across gantries until she is between the thunder runs above the stage—

installed, Portico said, to create *atmosphere*. The sound of thunder—wooden balls rolling—overhead.

Up amongst the retired exhibits, battered, broken things no longer fit for display, Allegra is humming. Her notes are discordant, like the ivory teeth of a piano knocked out of tune. She holds up a costume, her reflection scattered across the shattered mirror in front. On the wall hangs a poster, another long-dead ingenue in the very same dress. Where it once read *the Darling of the West End*, it now decrees *the Darling of the Deep, the Main Event*. Allegra's own features have been scribbled gracelessly over the ingenue's face. *Chosen Just for You.*

The air hangs so seedy-thick that Madrigal becomes herself a voyeur. She shouldn't be here. Creeping back between two gouged set pieces, Madrigal kicks a damaged spotlight and the thing spins and trembles. She clasps her hands over her mouth and shrinks behind a clutch of sagging dress stands.

"Hello?" calls Allegra. "Who's there?"

Madrigal leans away from the dancer's careful footsteps, edging closer—closer still.

"Is it you? Is it finally you? Have you come for me? I'm here—have you come?" Her voice is desperate, coarse as if she's scraping her long nails down her throat. The sound is so pitiful, so weak that Madrigal feels her lip shake.

When she slips away, she can still hear that question hanging like prayer.

"Have you come for me? I'm here—have you come?"

***

Bones sing in the dark.

Their mouths gape wide and gap-toothed, and strangled notes rattle out. She can see them in the darkness—bonedust aglow where the moonlight hits, creeping between the junk slats and into the museum. *Oh, here you are, a madrigal*, they chatter tunelessly. *When I gaze upon your face...*

Something touches her cheek, cold and clammy, and she lurches back—

and topples from the stool, scattering paintbrushes across her work bench. Paper, thick with ink, is stuck to her face. Madrigal smacks her lips and presses her eyes with her fingers.

Sleep. She must have fallen asleep.

She pulls the paper from her cheek. The image is smudged, but there is a figure still. *Oh, here you are.*

Madrigal squints in the dark—*the dark?*

She spins to the curtain, ruddy curls flailing like the seaweed beneath. The ghost light is unlit. Madrigal makes herself small and listens.

Nothing. Not the hum of the generator, nor even the biting sea.

She traipses blindly through the auditorium, running her hands across the wall until she feels a rounded door handle. *Below*, the wooden sign says. The door groans as she pushes it open and the sound of it makes her wince.

There are floors of the museum that sit beneath the waves, and as she slips down the stairs, Madrigal hears the acoustic blush of seawater coming in. Not quick enough to sink but enough to wet her feet and chill her legs to the bone. Down and down she goes until she hits the base of the museum. Here, the hulking generators are usually loud enough to deafen. Now, they sit silent.

The switch is big, stiff, and she has to haul all of her weight to shift it. It thunks against the wall. Still nothing, the generators remain dormant.

"What…" Madrigal listens but she cannot hear the regular scrape of the water wheel against the outer wall. "You've got to be joking."

Outside, rain lashes against the scrap, so thick that Madrigal cannot see where the sea ends and the night begins. She hugs her jacket close and pushes against the wind as it howls about her. The water wheel is still and when she shoves it, it resists.

"Something must be caught," she says, though the wind and the rain and the sea are so loud that she cannot hear herself. Strange, how quiet it seems within when a storm is roaring without.

It is too dark to swim so she thrusts her hand into the water and hopes. Her fingers catch something soft, yet stiff, and she tugs. When the thing comes loose she almost careens into the waves, catching herself on a lip of scrap.

She tightens her fingers and the thing squelches—*a ballet slipper?* Madrigal frowns and shoves it up her sleeve, her pocket filled at the seams with artistic accoutrements, now wet.

The water wheel sloshes back to life and so too do the generators, their mechanisms clunking across the storm.

Inside, though, nothing is illuminated. Outside, the museum's speakers burst to life. Madrigal feels her way back into the auditorium, tripping on bunched, waterlogged carpets.

Oh, here you are, a madrigal—oh, here, be mine to keep, lilts the voice so deep that it makes her knees shake. *Oh, here. Don't fuss, sweet madrigal, I'll hold you 'til the neap.*

Madrigal scrambles up to the stage, careful not to plunge into the empty orchestra pit. *Oh, should you run, or speak, or breathe— they'll rent us to the deep.* The voice is so close now that its cold breath caresses her ear—*oh, here you are, sweet madrigal. Don't hide, don't run. Don't run from me*—and the weight of its hand falls on her shoulder and then—

The ghost light flicks on, the hand is gone and there is Allegra—ashen, barefoot, and dripping—at the edge of the stage.

"You should have gone home," she says. "I can't help you now, when he comes."

"Portico?" Madrigal shifts her feet, moving backwards until she can feel the thick curtain.

Allegra laughs, hollow and rasping. "Portico Junk is a sap. A means to an end. A boy. *He* is the theatre, *he* is… It should be me. How did you catch him? What did you do? Why does he come for you? You! You shouldn't *be here. I* was chosen for him. You barely *look* the same."

She flings a hand out and Madrigal flinches. Photographs scatter like matrimonial confetti. The girl in the photograph has Madrigal's eyes. The similarity is not as uncanny as Allegra's—the dancer clenched in her fist could be her sister—but it is close enough that the hair on Madrigal's neck prickles.

"You should have gone home. Everything—everything that happens now is your doing. When he comes…" Allegra slides a balletic foot across the stage, and she dances towards the other girl. Swaying to her own keening notes. "It's all your fault."

Madrigal straightens her shoulders. Stands her ground. She slips the sodden shoe from her sleeve and holds it out to the dancer. "I think this belongs to you," says Madrigal without humour.

Rage hits Allegra like a hammer, and her face cracks wild. She shrieks and flies towards Madrigal, conch shell nails unsheathed and glinting. Her long arm catches the ghost light and the bulb crunches onto the stage. Allegra lets out a wail, from agony or anger, Madrigal cannot be sure.

She just knows she has to get out.

Oh, here you are, my madrigal—something clasps her coat and tugs. Madrigal wrenches free and leaves the garment behind, face smashing into the stage—*have it,* she thinks. She licks her lips and her tongue comes away bloody.

Oh, here you are—oh, come to me. Oh, come. Oh, come, my madrigal. The voice is everywhere, it booms and hums and sinks its teeth.

Somewhere behind, Allegra is incensed.

"I was meant to be yours. I was *meant* for you," she cries into the dark. When the voice quietens, she lilts, her own voice giddy and giggling, "Here you are, little Madrigal. Oh, yes. We're here at your behest—I'll take your heart into my hands and rip it from your chest."

The dancer cackles. Madrigal feels Allegra's breath hush against her cheek and runs—the curtains tangle around her, and squeeze. *Oh, come*, they sigh.

Madrigal wrestles through, scrapes her cheek on a loose nail, and hisses at the sting.

When I gaze upon your face, the voice resumes.

"Madrigal. Oh, Madrigal," sings Allegra. She's running something—her fingernails, or a knife, or the shattered glass of the ghost lamp—along the wall as she approaches.

Madrigal does not stop, does not dare to breathe until she reaches the box office. She barrels through the door and her feet meet something solid. The girl tumbles to the ground, the entire theatre bobbing in the salt. Something wet is beneath her hands, on her face, in her hair. It tastes like blood. So much blood.

"Portico?"

She cannot linger. The sing-song notes of the dancer have followed her down the hall. Soon she will be here—and there is only one way out. Madrigal scrabbles around in the dark until her fingers rest on cold metal. Paraffin.

She lugs the canisters out and looses their contents on the box office, the foyer, the wedge of scrap outside. Madrigal tears the oil lamp from the doorway and flings it into the entrance of the theatre.

The doorway blazes with light—though the fire burns white hot, the flames are cast a ghastly blue. Salt, just salt, though it looks as if it might be the cold breath of the dead leaping up from the sea below.

Flames eat their way up the scrap; they take the poster between crackling lips and swallow without chewing. *Theatreland on fire*, Madrigal thinks.

Over the spitting of the fire, the voice still sings—though soft, a quiet anger makes it tremble. *Why would you run from me? Oh, madrigal—you leave yet set my soul aflame.*

She douses the scrap behind her, chucking the canisters aside as she reaches the docks—*the docks!* Madrigal sweeps her wet curls from her face and scans the make-shift harbour for the boat.

Oh, run from me, sweet madrigal. Run and plunge into the sea...

Unmoored, the dinghy drifts. Through the thrashing rain, it looks a league away, thrown this way and that by the seething waves.

"No."

Behind her, the museum is swollen with cobalt flames and Allegra is screaming—she will never stop screaming. Madrigal covers her ears—she just wanted to go home, just as Allegra had said she should. *I'm sorry—*

The dock lurches, and she falls, catches, falls again, slipping towards the museum's flaming maw—Madrigal claws at the scrap and pulls herself to the edge, leaving a trail of bloodied nails behind her. She heaves herself over the lip and drops into the grey.

Oh, let the water in, my love—together we will be.

But the girl does not—she clamps her mouth shut and tries, tries, tries to keep from screaming. The ocean batters Madrigal, bites at her limbs, fills her up and threatens to drown her there in the cold blue light of the fire—she has to breathe.

The water cleaves at her throat, at her chest. If she could only breathe, just once more—just *once*.

A wave lifts her up and she gasps, the air sharp and piercing. She sucks in a breath and swims so hard her skin might rip from the effort of it. If she can just get to the boat.

She has been in the water forever; Madrigal does not remember what it is not to be swimming, heavy, when her hand hits wood. *The boat.*

With whatever is left of her strength, she hauls herself into the dinghy. She stays there in a heap, all ragged breath and coughing until the blue glow beckons her closer. Where there was once a museum, the blaze is blinding—from here, it is eerie cold. From across the sea, the fire whispers, *I'll follow you, sweet madrigal.*

Madrigal shivers.

Somewhere nearby, she imagines Allegra, scorched arms wide, eyes and mouth still open. The dancer, descending to the deep.

SELF STORAGE

by BARBARA A. BARNETT

"YOUR CREEPY DOLL COLLECTION IS FREAKING PEOPLE OUT," the sign outside Anderson's Self Storage reads. "STORE THEM HERE!"

Most drive by and laugh, if they notice the sign at all. But not Mia. She brakes, hard and sudden enough to elicit a screech of tires from the car behind her, the sustained belch of a horn, then a middle finger through the window. Mia registers it all the way she would a gnat, a tiny thing gone before she has time to consider swatting it.

It's the wording that draws her in: creepy. Not evil or possessed, because it's not like that. Just creepy.

She cuts off another car as she swerves into the parking lot, the next horn as distant as her ex's taunts about her normally too-too-careful driving.

Her foot twitches on the brake pedal. Coincidence? Delusion? She could slam down the gas, plow through the signboard, and determine just how real it is. No worse than what she'd been planning to do, right? Instead, she studies the sign more closely. Many of its changeable letters have gone missing. An upside down seven replaces one of the Ls in "DOLL"; a backwards three replaces the penultimate E of "HERE." Rust tinges the edges of the frame, and the grooves into

96

which the letters slide are caked with black crud.

Mia shuts off the engine. It's real. Had she dreamed up a sign, it would be immaculate, the letters perfectly spaced and all the same color. She's too fastidious to have produced this one, even in her imagination.

A day ago, she would have driven by and laughed, if she noticed the sign at all. Like most people. Today, she scrambles out of her car and hurries toward the rental office. The man at the desk is covered with liver spots and smells like cat hair and disease, yet Mia hugs him when they finish the paperwork. Her cheeks flush hot. God, she's never hugged anyone so spontaneously, not family, not a boyfriend.

She returns to her car, pops open the trunk, and lugs the first box of dolls toward a blocky, two-story building, inside which her new storage unit awaits.

Maybe this will stop her dreams about the river.

***

Sweat trickles down Steve's neck and winds through crevices beneath his shirt, as invasive as the sign's message: "THE SPORTS COLLECTOR'S CURSE: THEY'VE PLAYED MORE GAMES THAN YOU CAN FIT IN YOUR APARTMENT."

Coincidence, he thinks, loading his boxes onto a borrowed hand truck. He's the one with the dubious judgment, after all, choosing the middle of a heatwave to move an SUV's worth of baseball memorabilia—trading cards and pennants, bats and mitts, and the countless foul balls he caught in the stands as a kid.

Too many coincidences. Like the way those foul balls always came to him, no matter where he sat, no matter which ballpark. Yet of all the things his father's questioned about him over the years—his obsession with poetry, his lack of obsession with girls—the old man never questioned that. Just laughed and called his Steve-O an amazing catch, a natural, so why the hell had he quit playing ball himself?

Steve pushes the hand truck down an aisle inside Building #2. It's impossibly long, like the ones you traverse in a dream, with white concrete broken by red steel doors, each one grooved, padlocked, and identified by neat black numbers.

The hand truck's left wheel is loose, moving ever so slightly faster than the other. Steve piled the boxes too high, and now they teeter toward the right. He pushes the hand truck faster, the handles threatening to slip from his sweaty grasp. He should have buried the boxes in the middle of nowhere like he'd planned. A placard points the way toward his destination: Units 240-280.

Steve rounds the corner, and that's when he meets the girl with the dolls.

***

Mia doesn't hear footsteps or the squeaking wheel. It's not until the man with the hand truck speaks that she hears anything at all. His words are lost on her, even as they yank her back to consciousness.

She's standing in front of her storage unit, a doll at her feet, the door half open. Or is it half closed?

The man nods toward her hand. "You're bleeding."

She winces, partly from the cut on her finger, but more from having a stranger witness one of her disorienting returns to awareness. "The damn thing bit me."

His gaze flits between her and the doll at her feet: Beatrice, with her brown curls, frilly yellow dress, and porcelain lips pursed in a look of permanent dissatisfaction. The man's face goes so pale that Mia giggles.

"The door lock." She presses the edge of her t-shirt against the cut. "I caught my finger on it."

"Well, yeah, obviously it wasn't..." He fidgets, cheeks reddening as he adjusts his grip on the hand truck.

"Dude, if the doll bit me, you would have heard screaming. Lots and lots of screaming."

He responds with an unsteady laugh. Though he's half-obscured by the hand truck's tower of boxes, Mia sees enough to judge him in his late thirties like her, that age when you're supposed to be adult enough to have your shit together, yet you still feel like everything's out of your control.

Or is that just me?

He has the kind of easy handsomeness she's never gone for, but the edge to his laugh, the haunted way his gaze darts about— there's something off about him. Because he didn't just assume she was talking about the doll when she said the damn thing bit her. He would have *believed* it was the doll, she's sure of it.

He nods toward her hand again. "I have some band-aids back in my—"

He tilts the hand truck forward to set the lip on the floor; the bottom box crumples inward with a *whoomp*. They realize his mistake in unison—he swears and she darts forward—but neither is fast enough to stop the boxes from toppling. One bursts open and vomits its contents across the floor: hats, jerseys, and at least a dozen baseballs. Mia reaches for one.

"Don't!"

She flinches at his sharp tone, but her hand is already on the ball, holding it out to him. He stares, a twitch in his lower lip, as if she's offered him an unpinned grenade.

"It's just a ball," she says. "Right? I mean, unless you're smuggling drugs in it or something."

When he still doesn't take it, she mutters "whatever" and tosses it aside. Momentum should have carried it away from them, but instead the ball rolls toward the man's feet, where the other balls have accumulated as well. He kicks one away, grimaces as it rolls back.

Mia crouches to view the phenomenon at floor-level, feeling like a kid trying to figure out how the magic trick works. "How are you doing that?"

He snorts, then snatches up a ball and hurls it down the aisle, banking it off the wall so that it disappears around the corner. Another grimace.

"Okay, if you don't want to—"

"Wait for it."

The baseball reappears, rolling toward him. Mia giggles; it's like a dog faithfully padding back to its owner. But the way he looks at her in response—the watery eyes, arms clutched tight, like he's in pain. A man who really believed a doll had bitten her.

"It's not a trick," he says. "It's a fucking curse." He stares past her, into her storage unit. "Wanna tell me about yours?"

***

The girl's name is Mia, and the doll he so stupidly thought had bitten her is Beatrice. Steve didn't ask for the doll's name; Mia offered it without prompting. That would have been a normal person's cue to end the conversation. But he's not a normal person—*sorry, Dad*—and so her peculiarity holds him there like a magnet.

After stuffing his toppled collectibles back into the box—god, why did he show her what the balls did, he's never done that before—they sit in front of her storage unit, backs against either side of the open door. Inside the unit, boxes are neatly stacked as one might expect. In front of those boxes, as one might not expect, is a tea party: four dolls in Victorian gowns seated around a tiny pink table with a white doily and even tinier teacups.

"I black out sometimes," Mia says, never quite meeting his gaze, "and when I come to..." She nods toward the tea party. "My ex filmed me arranging them one time. I was...talking to them. Asking them questions, like where they wanted to sit. Can't blame him for leaving after that. It was creepy as fuck."

"When did you start collecting?"

Mia laughs, a jaded bark of a sound. "I never started. My parents gave me a few when I was a kid. And once you have a few, people assume it's a thing and keep getting them for you."

Steve chuckles. "Yeah, I know how that goes."

Mia plays with Beatrice's curls, pulling until they slip from her wispy fingers and spring back into place. "I hoped it would finally stop when I moved them here, but I keep coming back. One second I'm making a sandwich, the next I'm here."

She's much like her dolls: pale, round cheeks; glossy brown curls; a glassy cast to her eyes; her actions directed by some other hand.

"Lots of questions about me," she says. "So what's your story?"

Steve wrings his hands and decides a half-truth will suffice. "You saw it: the reason the guy who loves baseball is too scared to play."

"Is it, like, *every* baseball? I mean, if you're walking by a little league game, do all the balls just start rolling out of the equipment bag and following you down the street?"

Steve laughs—a good, satisfying, deep-from-the-gut one. "No, it's..." His next laugh is decidedly *not* satisfying, there to mask the shift in his mood as reality replaces her fanciful image. "It's not all of them. Just some."

There's more, and he wants to tell her, but the desire not to scare her away wins out. It always wins out.

"You came here because of the sign," she says.

He wrings his hands harder. It's not a question.

"There was something about sports on it today," she continues, "and you just happened to have all that shit in your car when you drove by, right?"

He shivers, not because of the AC blasting overhead, but because of coincidences that aren't really coincidences. "Same for you?"

She nods, stands, then surveys her storage unit, as if considering how best to set fire to it. Maybe she should; maybe he should help. Instead, Mia unleashes a shriek and hurls Beatrice at the tea party. The other dolls topple from their chairs. They hit the ground with dress-muffled taps, out of place with the clatter of their plastic teacups.

Mia leans forward, hands on her knees, breathing like someone who's just run a marathon. "I hate this fucking place."

Her finger is bleeding again, which makes Steve think of the lock, which in turn gives him an idea. It's so simple.

"We can trade keys," he says. "To our storage units. Then you can't get to the dolls, the balls can't get to me, and we're both free."

Before he's even finished speaking, she's rummaging through the purse she wears slung over one shoulder.

"Just one condition," Steve adds. "Don't touch my shit, and I won't touch yours. We just let it all collect dust and move on with our lives."

Mia finds her key and thrusts it in his face. "It's a deal, ball boy."

***

More than Mia's finger is bleeding now. Her knuckles are bruised and split open, the skin around them smeared in sunset shades of purple and red. Her fingernails are ragged and broken. She has no memory of trying to claw her way into the storage unit, yet the evidence is there, etched into the door's fluted red metal.

Shouldn't the noise have drawn someone?

She lifts her hands to her mouth, licks away the salty blood, and laugh-cries in gratitude for the pain. It's the only reason she's snapped back to consciousness.

Shouldn't there be a guard? Some blue-uniformed guy who knows every unit renter by name?

Her hand aches, yet she forces it into her purse and fumbles out her phone. 2:34 a.m.

How the hell did I get in here? The gate closes at 10.

She doesn't remember texting Steve, but she's sent him at least ten messages, asking for his address and never getting a response.

Her breathing quickens—sharp inhale, staccato quaver on the exhale, repeated like a drum beat. What the hell had she been thinking, trusting her key to some rando without getting more than a cell number? Not even a last name. Maybe he stole her shit. Maybe there's nothing behind that door.

No. The dolls are here because she's here. Like that time after her fifth grade slumber party, when Stephanie Miller snuck one home with her. Mia had no idea who'd taken it, yet she jumped on her bike and rode straight to Stephanie's house, the same feeling then as tonight: thoughts clouded, body numb. Only that pull. No, that *yank*. Coming to her senses in a strange house, one she'd apparently stormed into without knocking, and Stephanie Miller crying and saying she didn't want her stupid doll anyway, and the other kids always whispering after that even though Mia doesn't remember scratching Stephanie's cheek.

Mia leans against the wall and slides to the floor. Her t-shirt drags against the concrete and she wants to rip the damn thing off. Because she doesn't remember getting dressed, she only remembers... well, not these clothes. She never would have paired this shirt with these sandals. One of her broken nails catches on the shirt, and now there's blood on it, wet like the river.

She'd been dreaming of the river again. Dreaming of drowning.

Even dead I'd still be here clawing at the door. Zombie girl needs her dolls.

She shifts, feels the jab of something hard and pointed in her back pocket. Steve's key.

Don't touch my shit, and I won't touch yours.

Well, fuck that promise. Because she wouldn't be such a middle-of-the-night shitshow if it weren't for his brilliant idea, now, would she?

Mia's breathing evens. She stands and heads toward Unit 276.

***

"My ex filmed me...talking to them. Asking them where they wanted to sit."

When the knocking starts, Steve's already awake, scribbling out a poem that will remain hidden in a notebook with all the others. Poetry isn't a thing guys like him are supposed to be into. Feelings are a thing you're supposed to keep hidden lest people find the stitching holding you together. Lest they dig their fingers between the seams and tear.

He knows it's Mia at the door. He's ignored her texts because that's what she asked him to do when they swapped keys: *If I know where you live, I'll totally stalk you to get it back.* But she's found his address after all, and worse, he knows she went through his storage unit. That's the reason he's awake, a bandage on his forearm, red splotching through the gauze.

Bitch can wait.

But his head throbs in time with her knocking, a maddening synchronicity that finally drives him to his feet, notebook tossed aside. He yanks open the door. "What?"

Mia lowers the hand that had been pounding. The red and purple swell of her knuckles is the only reason he doesn't tell her to fuck off. He doesn't need to ask how they got that way.

She follows his stare. "Do you have an ice pack or something?"

Steve snorts. As if that's why she's here. Yet he waves her inside.

"What'd you do to your arm?" she asks.

He heads to the kitchen, no answer, no invitation to sit. Just leaves her standing in his living room. When he returns with a towel-wrapped ice pack, she's spinning in circles, studying his walls and shelves. With her oversized purse weighing down one shoulder, she looks like a lopsided merry-go-round horse. Her gaze breezes past photos, artwork, and his piles of books, lingering instead on the empty spaces where the sports memorabilia had been.

"You're lucky I don't have to work in the morning." He thrusts the ice pack at her. "You wanna tell me how you got my address?"

Mia shrugs. "I had you pegged for the former Boy Scout type. Figured you'd have neat little labels with your contact info affixed to the back of your stuff. And I was right."

He clenches his jaw. It's all he can do not to snatch the ice pack away.

"Don't worry." Mia eyes his rumpled t-shirt and boxers,

smirking. "I didn't touch any of your magic balls."

"Except you did."

"Look," she says, "just give me my key back already."

"No."

She twitches like an addict. "What the fuck, man?"

"We had an agreement—no going through each other's shit—and you broke it."

"Because I need my key."

She stares at him, eyes bloodshot, lower lip trembling. She shifts the ice pack from hand to hand until the towel unravels. It falls to the floor, the ice pack follows, and then her tears. It's such a pathetic display that all Steve can think about is how damp his carpet will get. He reaches for the ice pack, but she grasps him by the shirt.

"Please, I'll do anything you want, anything you like."

She presses close, lips parted. Steve cringes even though she's the one who should be embarrassed. As if he's supposed to be enticed by this: her battered, ice cold hands; her hair hanging in tangled clumps; her bulky purse knocking against his thigh.

He eases her away. "There are so many reasons why that isn't going to happen."

Mia's gaze finally falls on something other than the empty spots on his shelves: the photo of him and Jason, hand in hand outside a stadium.

"Boyfriend?" she asks.

"Yeah."

"But he's not here now?"

The way she says it—Christ, he can't tell if she's thinking she might still be able to seduce him or if she's insinuating that his relationship sucks. Not that she'd be wrong about the latter. Too afraid of opening up, too afraid of getting hurt, too afraid of being himself—Jason has an infuriatingly accurate litany of things Steve's afraid of. But right now lying is easier than admitting they broke up, so he mutters, "Night shift at the hospital."

"Doctor?"

"Nurse."

What, not smart enough to be a doctor? his father once said, yet in the same breath remained perplexed as to why Steve wouldn't bring Jason over to meet him.

Mia's interest shifts from the photo to the jacket draped over the arm of his couch. She peers closely at the union seal emblazoned on the front, like she's going to sniff it. "United steelworkers? So is that what you—"

"I'm not giving you the key."

She sighs and turns her gaze upwards, as if making some last-ditch appeal to a higher power. He *should* give her the key. He should get his own back and be done with this drama of his own creation. But just like when they met, he senses some kind of thread between them.

No coincidences. He's sure of that.

"Look," Mia says, "you seem like a decent guy, but..."

She reaches into her purse, and Steve tenses. She has one of his baseballs. "Mia, give me—"

"Your creepy-ass ball?" She turns it until he can see the loose stitching and the small flap of white leather peeling away, no cork or rubber core beneath, instead a pulsing mass of veins and scarlet-drenched muscle. "I just obsessively arrange dolls, but this? This is a special kind of fucked up."

The way she wrinkles her nose suggests disgust as much as confusion. She hasn't made the connection yet, he realizes. The calmness of that observation somehow coexists with the cold sweat drenching him.

"Give me back my key," Mia says, "and I'll give you back your ball. Though honestly?" She fingers the loose leather flap, and he shudders. "Why you'd want this back is beyond me. I mean—"

"Don't—"

But she's already peeling back the leather, exposing more of the fleshy mass beneath, and his own skin tears with it. He screams. The same pain that jolted him out of bed earlier now drops him to his knees. He clasps a hand over his arm, but the blood is too fast, it's on the carpet with the thawing ice pack, and absurdly, he laughs through the pain at noticing that.

"Jesus!" Mia drops the ball. The exposed section strikes the floor, and Steve howls again, the nerves in his arm on fire. "I didn't realize..."

His neighbor bangs on the wall and barks out indistinct words that seem to assume screams of pleasure, not pain. Steve's now-useless bandage dangles beside the length of skin torn off with it. He tugs the bandage free and bites hard into his lip, as much to keep from whimpering as to keep from passing out.

Mia kneels beside him, grabs the discarded towel, and presses it over his arm. "I wouldn't have...I didn't realize..."

"Why the hell would you?" he says through clenched teeth. "You just obsessively arrange dolls, like a normal freak."

She flinches, her shoulders sink, and all he can think is good, he's hurt her now too. Even though he was right: how *would* she know? It's not the kind of thing you guess—there's something alive beneath the skin of those balls, a part of you, and you can't get rid of it no matter how hard and far you throw it.

And that's the problem, he realizes, staring at the blood-soaked towel on his arm, then at Mia's bruised hands holding it in place. Trying to get rid of their respective curses is how they ended up here, isn't it?

His pain is subsumed by a calm so sudden that he wonders if he's going into shock.

They've been going about it all wrong.

***

Mia's never cared for wine—too bitter, even the sweet stuff, and it always leaves her with a headache. But it's the only alcohol Steve has, and her head has been throbbing for hours already, so it's what she drinks while he cleans himself up in the bathroom.

The baseball sits on the coffee table now, wedged between two thick poetry collections, the leather smoothed back into place. No, *smoothed* isn't the right word, because fucking hell, that noise it made, that *slurp* as it reconnected with the sinew underneath.

Mia's wine reverses direction, burning up her throat, and she swallows it back. Christ, that thing had been jostling around in her purse, and before that she'd been poking at it in Steve's storage locker, treating it like a high school biology lab dissection.

How could I have known?

Steve returns from the bathroom, a new patch of gauze taped to his forearm. He cocks his head and scrutinizes the carpet—damp, but no longer bloody—then the formerly crooked-hanging Van Gogh print she straightened, then the notebook she moved from his armchair to the side table, then the other books on his shelves, now in neat stacks where before they'd resembled a game of Jenga.

"So it's not just the dolls with you," he says.

"You should see how neat your storage unit is now." Mia tries to laugh, but the sound is like a deflating tire. It's not the same with the dolls. Tidying up his stuff was a choice.

Steve collapses into a chair, a hideous orange-red she associates with vomit, and that's when she notices how pristine white his bandage is. At least he's not bleeding so profusely anymore.

"Does it still hurt?" she asks.

"Clarity is one hell of an anesthetic."

"Clarity?"

A moment ago, Mia would have described the look on his face as distant, but now she notices the slight upward turn at the corners of his mouth. Not quite a smile, but close.

"Where were you going when you saw the storage place sign?" he asks.

Mia takes a too-big gulp of wine. Through the tight-chested burn, she mumbles a lie about meeting a friend for drinks. Then she cringes and waits for him to call her on her bullshit, because why the hell would she have a trunkful of dolls for that? But he doesn't push her; he doesn't even look at her.

"I was going to find a spot in the middle of the woods and bury it all," he says, staring straight ahead with that not-quite-a-smile. "It wouldn't have worked, though. Pile all that dirt on top and I'd probably start suffocating."

It's unnerving the way he won't look at her, making her feel like the child of an inattentive parent—*look at me, Mom, I'm gonna jump, MOM YOU'RE NOT LOOKING*—and so she blurts out the truth: "I was going to dump mine over the side of Newfield Bridge, right into the middle of the fucking river."

"You know you would have blacked out and gone wading in after them, right?"

"That was the point, yeah."

His face drops, and she can't believe he's never considered that way out of his situation before.

"Huh."

Huh? *There's* her rage again. That single, dismissive syllable is like a stoking of embers, prodding her fire back to life. She chugs the last of her wine, sets the glass down too hard on the table, and clambers to her feet. Was that seriously all the consideration her life warranted? A *huh*?

"Thanks for the wine, asshole."

She heads for the door, and ridiculously she's thinking of how she didn't leave the glass on a coaster, how a small bit of purplish-red wine is trickling down the side.

"Mia," Steve says, standing.

She turns, and he's holding out his hand, palm up. Her key. Christ, her only reason for coming here and she'd almost left without it.

"Locking this shit away isn't working," he says. "I think it's time we stop hiding it."

She's about to tell him he's gone loopy from the blood loss, but a photo on the wall behind him catches her eye: Steve and a bunch of other hard-hatted men drinking from thermoses. The massive, skeletal structure rising around them makes them look as tiny as dolls.

And she has an idea.

***

Steve spies Mia swatting at gnats as she walks toward the baseball field, for once empty of little league games and the local amateur softball league. He almost didn't invite her, but then he got her text and the photos of what she'd done with the dolls.

You were right, she'd written. *Not hiding this shit, you were so fucking right.*

Easy for her to say. Her brand of fucked up was something you could embrace without hurting yourself. But his—well, his stemmed from a lifetime of trying *not* to get hurt.

Time to try the opposite approach now.

He stands at home plate, bat in one hand, the baseballs scattered at his feet. Mia's walking along the right field side of the chain-link fence. Jason's approaching from the left field side, clad in green scrubs that suggest a stop to or from work. And Steve's father is squinting at him through the rusty silver crisscross of the backstop. Always too stubborn to wear his glasses.

"Steve?" His father glances up and down from his phone, clearly trying to puzzle out the cryptic text message that brought him here. "What's going on?"

Steve picks up a ball, tosses it into the air, and swings. He winces at the sharp crack of ball-against-wood. The ball lands between second and third base, stirring up a dirty cloud of dust. The cloud settles, the ball stays put, and for a moment he hopes he won't have to go through with this. But then it starts rolling back.

"You wanna know why I really stopped playing, Dad?" He hits another one and feels the impact like a kick to the back of his knee. He staggers, but shakes off the pain and scoops up the next ball. "It wasn't because I hated it like I told you. I loved it, actually."

His father just stands there, mouth agape. Jason's gotten closer, but his steps are slower. Hesitant. Mia, though, is running. Because she knows.

"But I also had this crush on one of my teammates," Steve says. Another swing, another hit, and this one feels like a rib snapping in his chest. "Andy Evans. Him and the other guys found this poem I'd written about him—damn notebook fell out of my bag after practice—and they..."

Toss, swing, crack. Bruises have blossomed on his arms and legs, red-purple blobs the size of his fists. Much like that day after practice. He reaches for another ball. The ones on the field roll back, like some sort of surreal stampede.

"Remember that day I came home looking like I'd been in a fight, and I told you I'd taken a spill on my bike? Yeah, that was bullshit. But I think you knew that."

Mia's reached the opening between the fence and the backstop. "Don't—"

He drowns out her protest with another crack of the bat. His lip splits open.

"I knew you'd say it was my fault I got my ass kicked." He wipes the blood from his mouth. "Because you were always telling me to toughen up and be a man, so that's what I did."

Mia rushes up to him and tries to snatch the bat away, but he shoves her off, hard enough that she falls on her backside in the dirt.

"Stop letting people see who you are underneath," he says, "and you don't get hurt." He grabs another ball—the one where the white leather is pulling apart from the stitching. "Turns out that theory's bullshit too."

The ball in the air, the crack of the bat, a tearing of flesh. He screams, his body feels like it's on fire, and there's shouting around him as he drops to the ground. But just before he passes out, he sees the ball land by the center field fence, and he laughs.

Because this time, it doesn't roll back.

***

Mia doesn't black out anymore, and she no longer dreams about the river.

Sometimes she dreams about the baseball field; only, in the dream, *all* of Steve's skin tears off, yet somehow he's still holding the bat and the ball, nothing but bloody muscle as he takes his next swing and smiles at her with too-white teeth.

Those are the nights when she wakes up in a sweat and dry-heaves in the bathroom, when it takes her a few minutes to remember it didn't really happen that way.

What Mia's never dreamed about is being an artist. Yet that's what everyone calls her arrangements of the dolls: pop-up art. Installations that appear in the middle of the night, in random spots around town, set up by an anonymous creator.

Some people think the installations are haunted, because there's always some jackass who steals a doll or pockets a plastic tea-cup, and of course she knows where to find them. She likes to imagine each thief's reaction when they learn the purloined item has mysteriously reappeared at the installation with a note declaring, "The gentleman who lives at 124 Smith Street stole me." Her perverse little pleasure.

"You're like the Banksy of creepy dolls," Steve says.

She's brought him to her latest installation: several of her dolls seated along the eaves of a local brewery with beer cans in place of teacups.

Other people have gathered as well, snapping pictures. Mia's grin widens. None of them have a clue the artist is standing among them. None except Steve, and having someone who understands why she does this is even stranger than her anonymous fame. A friend—the word feels weird considering everything, but that must be what they are now. Because friends are the people who drive you home from the hospital. Friends are the people who forgive you for scaring them.

The bandages covering Steve's skin grafts are too numerous not to stare at—on his neck, on his legs, on his arms. And those are only the ones she can see. As he follows her back to her car, a Frankenstein-like lumber to his steps, he talks about the conversations he had in the hospital with Jason and his father.

"Things got pretty ugly, but..." He tries to shrug, but only one shoulder seems willing to cooperate, making the gesture look more like a nervous tic. "At least we're talking things out now."

"Without the gory theatrics, I hope?"

"Yeah, I wanted to show you..." He opens the rear door of her car and reaches into the box on the backseat, full of the baseballs she collected from the field.

He tosses one away; it doesn't roll back.

"I think I'm gonna leave it there," he says, smirking as he climbs into the passenger seat.

On the drive to his apartment, he's reading her one of his poems when she slows the car to a crawl. Luckily, no one's behind her to lay on the horn. Not like the day she slammed on the brakes in this same exact spot.

Steve starts cracking a joke about her old lady driving habits, but she hushes him and points to the new sign outside Anderson's Self Storage: "YOU'RE GOING TO NEED MORE SPACE FOR YOUR RECORDS NOW THAT VINYL'S HIP AGAIN."

In the parking lot, a paunchy, balding man has just finished loading boxes onto a hand truck. He closes the trunk of his car, then casts a wary gaze up at the sign.

Mia glances at Steve, who doesn't believe in coincidences.

"It's like this place collects collectors," he says.

"Fellow freaks." She smiles. "Should we learn what his deal is?"

Steve nods, and Mia pulls her car into the lot.

NUDE IN REPOSE #37

by HARKLIN ASHE

Toni took one look at the man standing near the foot of her bed and pegged him as a hangover from a dream she'd already forgotten. His profile reminded her of a saxophone. He arched back as though balancing a bowling ball on his chest. His pelvis yearned forward.

His ridiculous silhouette distracted Toni for a few breaths, then clarity closed her throat. While the sax man's body pointed toward the wall, his eyes ran over her skin.

Toni wrenched up. He was real. She was naked, in a strange bed, in a strange room filled with people strolling around, pretending to peruse paintings, projections, and curios while their eyes flicked over her.

She groped for a sheet, a blanket, a tassel-happy accent pillow. Nothing. The lumpy mattress expelled notes of chlorine as she squirmed, peeking over the side.

The barren floor slapped her. No clothes, no purse, no phone. She tossed across the bed and found the same buffed floor, as empty as her memory of last night.

She couldn't imagine what she'd done. Never, even after her roughest nights, had she misplaced her purse, her phone, and her clothes; at least not all at once.

Unwilling to face the sax man or the swarming strangers, Toni focused on the floor until the granite's flecks started dancing. Her stomach acid roiled and seeped into her memory. She saw Sazerac in a cut glass, smelled bitter anise, and tasted whiskey.

Toni retched. Instead of exorcising bile, her sea-lion bark gave everyone an excuse to stare openly.

Time froze. She stopped breathing. She kept still while her inner body twisted like a sponge, wringing out her humiliation's signature musk of sour peaches and sea brine. The sax man broke the stillness. He stepped closer and smiled. His quivering teeth looked hungry.

Toni stumbled off the bed. Her eyes darted around the gallery's anemic columns and mesh panels. No doors or windows. Nowhere to hide, except in the crowd.

She chose the mob's scattered interest over the sax man's intimate observation. When enough bodies barricaded his probing eyes, she folded over, bracing for another retch but getting a belch instead. The previous night's revenant flavor woke more memories.

She saw teasing lips, as suggestive as arched brows. Her goosebumps rose for the spectral thumb painting her forearm with martini-glass dew. Her ears rang with the line she'd received instead of a name.

"Anonymity is a true artist's canvas."

Those words had magnetized her. Now they repulsed her.

The crowd swirled faster. One last memory surfaced. She bowed lower, pressing her hands into the floor, but the cold granite couldn't temper the burning realization that she'd walked right into the trap.

She'd been flattered to hear the artist wanted to use her in a piece and neglected to ask what kind.

Beyond that moment, her memory atrophied into a blur fueled by alcohol and possibly other influences. She remembered nothing about arriving or being at the gallery. Scanning the room through the crowd made her dizzy, but she persisted and eventually found something familiar, a face she couldn't believe she'd forgotten.

She drifted toward her friend. The crowd disappeared. Nothing existed but the black curls ineffectively trussed in a chignon and the spirit ineffectively bound by a frame engraved with the name, "Viola."

"Anonymity is a true artist's canvas."

The tease in the lifelike portrait's asymmetrical smile, the s-curve in her spine, suggested a nude despite her plum gown. The dress dangled from Viola's shoulder, but her aspect insinuated complete control over the garment.

Daytime's harsh light brought Viola's indigo eyes to life. They harbored a campfire gleam Toni had seen many times, always before hearing a secret. She traced Viola's conspiratorial gaze across the wall—over postmodern triptychs and Bauhaus imitations—to the bed she never wanted to see again.

Shame warmed her cheeks, but she couldn't tear her eyes off something she noticed from this new vantage; something behind her bed, barely visible on the white wall. She stepped closer, squinting, to make out an artwork label reading, *Kye, Nude in Repose #37.*

Kye. Toni thanked Viola with a bow. Now she had a name. She had most of a face. She had enough.

Determination eclipsed self-consciousness. Toni studied the faces surrounding her, but instead of finding anyone who might be Kye, she found a jacket abandoned on a modular settee just paces away.

She pounced on it, hugging the wool to her chest. Her flesh shuddered and relaxed enough to make exposure chafe anew when a man clawed the jacket away.

"Please."

The man brushed Toni aside and strode off. She watched, waiting for him to put on the jacket, knowing he wouldn't. He did, however, walk through a wall.

She hacked her way through limbs wrapped in fleece, leather, and denim to reach the hidden opening, an archway leading to a different gallery. The jacket clutcher strode across it and eventually disappeared through yet another archway into yet another gallery.

It was a maze.

A woman surveying a feathered mask goosenecked her concentration onto Toni. The fresh attention pushed her back into the familiar room filled with familiar stares. She pressed her face against a bare wall and ignored everything.

Her clammy skin had almost fused to the paint when she felt a warm breeze. It cloaked the air conditioning's chemical odor with aromas of wet cardboard and celery.

Fresh air.

What usually smelled like nothing now seemed as pungent as a rose. She tracked the scent across the gallery to find one tile in a lemon-grove mural swinging out to let sunlight stream in.

Toni ran, generating energy with each step. Nothing could slow her down, not even the old woman she bumped or the glass pedestal she shattered.

She lingered before the door, savoring the dusty heat and the eye-scorching light. A minivan bounced past and interrupted her reverie. Looking through its bruise-tinted windows, Toni could see an entire family ogling her.

She let the door close. Beyond it lay strange stares, cars full of them, busses full of them. Leaving the maze didn't mean escaping. It would keep her bound as long as she wore nothing, had nothing, and owned nothing, including her body.

Toni collapsed, defeated, onto the base of a humanoid sculpture spun from metal wires. Art enthusiasts sharked around her, but she just held still, wanting the feeding over as quickly as possible. Her fight rekindled when the sax man glided forward for a private audience. She crawled between the sculpture's wiry legs, but they couldn't block his hot breath, couldn't stop him from inspecting her like a dog-show judge.

She searched the crowd for any helpful or kind face but found no human warmth until the bodies parted just enough to let Viola shine through.

Imagining Viola's arms guiding her, Toni uncoiled from beneath the sculpture. She mimicked Viola's posture. She let her legs fall in a careless pile instead of squeezing them tight. She let her spine curve, let her flesh unfurl.

Reveling in the pose's power, Toni understood Viola's second secret: She didn't have control over her plum gown. She just didn't care if it slipped off.

For the first time since waking up in the strange bed, Toni smiled. She faced the sax man and stretched, offering her body before he could take it. Her confidence flared as his hungry fire sputtered, dimmed, and finally died.

Watching him slink away, Toni knew no scrutiny, however strange or lewd, could touch her.

"Ma'am?"

Toni flinched, blinking around, eventually matching the voice to a man with hearth-warm eyes and a curly gray halo.

"Umgh?"

"I'm sorry to bother, or disturb you, I mean, but I was hoping you might know where I can find Kye."

Arrested by the name, Toni just stared. She found words when she noticed the man fidgeting with a press badge.

"You can't find Kye?"

"Sadly no. I'm told they like to remain anonymous. Impossible to reach. But people are raving about this, this…"

The man's eyes stuttered over Toni's chest and snapped closed. He took a deep breath.

"They're raving about this show. Perfect time to own the moment. Finally do that debut interview, you know?"

The word "own" filled Toni with a velvet warmth that bloomed into an idea.

"So you've never met Kye?"

"Nope."

"Ever seen a photo?"

"Doubt they even exist." The man shrugged. "Kye's a mystery, says 'Anonymity is a true artist's canvas.' "

The words that had first magnetized her and then repulsed her now invigorated her.

Lips curling into Viola's smile, eyes agleam, Toni leaned forward. The man mirrored her as though she had him on a rope. She tasted her whisper before blowing it into the reporter's ear.

"I'm Kye."

JUNK SOUL

by LAUREN BOLGER

It wasn't a junkyard in the sense most understood the word. Becky came to Margie Pearlman's property only after blowing through her entire paycheck on Tennessee whiskey and running out of anything else she could sell. It was the perfect place to get scrap metal in a pinch.

Lately, the visits were more frequent.

To Becky, they were *almost* the worst thing on earth, second only to spending too much of her weekend sober. She stopped by the rusted old motorcycle hoisted nine feet off the ground by a mature tree; a tree which was fully uninterested in the hunk of metal that had dared to impede its growth however-many years ago. The entire front axle had separated from the rest of it, and it lay on the ground nearby, front tire still in tow, riddled with all manner of mushrooms.

She stared at it and thought about organic things and slow decimation; the fierce violence that pulsed from that severed tire. A chorus of crickets rattled angrily at her feet.

Fourteen-odd vehicles littered old Pearlman's property in all forms of disrepair, some doorless with moss clinging to the windshield, others only bare metal frames, all tires flat and sunken in the dirt. The state got involved when two or more non-driveable cars were left on a property. It had to be registered as a junkyard. That, or the cars had to be removed.

"Or what?" Becky asked. An owl hooted somewhere nearby. Her heart hammered. Every step deeper into the junkyard made her weaker with doubt. Becky wanted so badly to turn back, but there was no money left. No food in the fridge. Leaving would be admitting defeat and sitting at home, hungry, sober, and alone.

"It'll be worth your while tonight, honey," a dead guttural voice came from deep inside her.

Quick and cold, something invisible bloomed in her gut.

"God!" she hissed through her teeth. "You scared me!"

"You'll never get used to that, will you?"

"I'm sure it'll take more than a few weeks to get used to a voice coming from inside my body. It'd help if you didn't wait until I was alone in a darkened junkyard to start talking to me."

"That's not up to me."

"You don't ever answer my questions, so I won't bother to ask what that means."

"What's there to know? I'm a voice that comes from inside you."

Becky shook her head. "What's there ta know," she grumbled. "Plenty, you fucker."

"I wouldn't call me that."

Becky's anger curdled, and fear took over. Her eyes watered. "Sorry." She bit her lip, took a few deep breaths, swallowed her leaping heart, and kept walking. Each step carried her closer to the broad, white moon. A turtle shell, picked clean to the bone by the tides of time. The speckled aged thing gaped at her from behind wretched black branches, feeling impossibly close.

Play nice, she warned herself. "What do you call yourself anyway? You won't tell me your name. So how about a nickname?" Thinking she saw something shiny, she peered in one of the rusted-out cars. Both of its doors were broken and hanging open. Nothing there. Just a lone shard of windshield catching the moonlight.

"You won't find anything in there. Getting warmer, though," the voice said. "You can call me Papa."

"Papa, like Dad?" She veered over towards a maroon Taurus station wagon. Rust had climbed over the wheel wells until the metal was eaten away, leaving them grinning, jagged and jawless.

"No, like 'potato' in Spanish," the voice said sarcastically.

"Yeah, like Dad. I'm your anti-parent. Getting colder, by the way."

She turned away and continued down the messy aisle of cars. "Anti-parent? Then why not go backwards? You could be Apap. Also, I always thought you were female."

"Why?"

"I don't know. It's hard to tell, really. Your voice is very… flat. But you call me honey."

"I'm a parasite attached to your soul, Becky. Gender doesn't actually come into play here."

Her heart dropped. A soul parasite. That didn't sound familiar, or good. Her breath quickened. "Ok, Papa."

"You can call me Mama if it makes you happy. Up ahead, to the right."

Becky looked right. Something at the pit of her stomach clenched, then pulled her hard in that direction. She stumbled forward and fell to her knees, pain shooting up her legs. A *new* old car sat there; its presence combing back the tall grass. A gray Datsun. Sweat crept out of her pores. Her face felt cold.

"Not feeling so hot, huh? You see the car I found you?"

Becky swiped a palm over her face. "*You* found it?"

The Datsun sat in the center of a scattered circle of other fully collapsed cars, creepers wound around the tires, grasses bursting straight through the cabins and spilling out the windows. The outer cars had clearly been there much longer.

As if the Datsun had just appeared there one day.

"How?"

"Go ahead, get inside."

The pull in her stomach got stronger, sharper. She cried out, doubling over, hugging herself.

"Trust me," it said.

Another tug. Pain leapt up her midsection, brought her up on one knee.

"I can't," she admitted. Tears stung her eyes. "It hurts."

"I was trying to do this the easy way, Becky. I think you know this is a command, not an invitation."

What would it do to her if she didn't listen? "Funny. I used to think you were helping me," she whispered. The tears crept down her cheeks, gathering on her chin.

Hands shaking, she stood and stepped slowly towards the vehicle. Why did it want her to go there so bad?

She drew closer still. The car wasn't gray, it was baby blue. Her vision sharpened. Why was it so familiar to her? Her breath came ragged and fast. Memories hung like storm clouds; caged electricity threatening to crash over her. In her mind, she pictured herself getting in, and the car reversing on its own. She wouldn't be able to stop it. To control it.

"No." This wasn't *that* car. It couldn't be. Her eyes watered again. "I don't wanna get in."

"Get in." Its voice, which had always been flat before, was steely now. Threatening.

Again, she chose the second worst thing. She got in. The inside of the car smelled like old vinyl. Like a camping tent stored for too long.

"Shut the door."

Becky cried from deep inside herself, her body wrenched by each sob. Her insides were sore, like they were fighting letting it out. Her hair hung over her tear and snot-covered face. She pressed the heels of her hands against her eyes, took a deep breath, and held it, shutting the door. Her head ached, and her ears rang like she'd been bashed in the head.

***

She heard it now. The pounding on the back window. She was half-drunk, moving her friend's car. She'd turned around to back up and there was Seth, shouting threats at her. She'd clunked into reverse and floored the gas. Ran him over, and he was gone, just like that.

Still, like a bird that'd bashed into a window.

His body broken, neck bent, mouth bleeding. His mom saw that, but not the murderous glint in his eyes right before she did it. Becky got off, but not without being hated by everyone she knew.

***

"Becky, Becky, Becky."

"God! *What?* Stop saying my name like that." Somehow, she was sitting in the car that'd killed Seth.

"You made a little split inside yourself and chased your bad feelings away. That's where I crawled in. I found the place where you left yourself behind."

"This *fucking* car." Becky grabbed the wheel and tried to get back out, but that force in her stomach held her down like a seatbelt. She tried to cry out, but her first sob wrenched all the breath from her lungs. She wished she had someone, anyone who'd come looking for her. *My friends. They left me. They left me because of him.*

Since then, she'd poured herself into work during the week, then drank the weekends away.

I left me too, she realized.

She opened her eyes again. There was a face under the steering wheel. Wide eyed, jaw stretched open as if in absolute shock. It was her, her face exactly, except with bright white skin, black smudges around the eyes, and an impossible mane of straw-like brown hair, longer than she'd ever had it.

With a heave, she scrambled backwards between the front seats and launched herself into the second row. Shoving to the side, she tried one of the doors. Locked. Of course.

"That face. You're how I felt," she whispered. "You're how I felt that night."

As if that's what other-Becky was waiting to hear, two long-armed thin bony hands grasped the center console, its ghoulish face gradually rising; a shining death moon. It grasped her thighs and pulled itself up slowly, deliberately, making eye contact at the same time. It brought its lips to hers as if to kiss her. "You're me. You can't hurt me," she whispered once, then repeated it again, eyes squinting, mouth clamped shut. "You're me. You can't hurt me," pressing the words out the side of her mouth.

The thing moved its hands up, pressed fingers into her mouth, and pulled it open.

"Aaaah!" Her breath came fast now, in short little gasps. *She's me, she can't hurt me,* she thought in her head, trying to force herself to breathe deep, breathe slow.

Maybe it'd hurt, but it couldn't last.

***

She opened her eyes but couldn't see anything. Where had the moon gone? Was she blind? Blinking rapidly did nothing. She lay there a few minutes, hoping her eyes would adjust.

There was a foreign, yet familiar feeling in her midsection. Warm, sticking to her ribs, like a comfort meal. She cried now, but it was a necessary cry. It hurt like a good workout does. Like improvement. The warmth spread itself like jelly, sticking to the coldness inside. The coldness she'd nursed for eight months each time she'd visited this wasteland.

She wanted to heal, but the cold and the warmth revolted, one against the other, stirring savagely in her stomach. The pain was sharp and continuous. Becky gagged violently, her eyes wide and watering. She held as still as she could but that last swipe of warmth had bent her over.

Again, she focused on breathing.

Eventually, a faint glow bled into her peripheral. The warm voice spoke, rougher than the cold one. "You left me here to die. And in my place, became this junkyard rat."

"I didn't know it would happen," she cried. "I need you. I'll fix this."

"No. *We* will fix this. I'll tell you where to cut."

Becky turned her head towards the glow. A small hatchet lay on the floor of the backseat. A little Sportsman's axe. Blond wood handle with little stripes. New, shiny, clean.

The glowing blade sang a wordless song. Older than the old cars. Older than all the trees in the forest.

WE NAMED YOU AFTER HER

by RACHEL UNGER

It was just as well that the driver dropped Lee early—they'd closed the road past the Bi-Lo grocery parking lot, cordons pressed into what had to be a foot of displaced sand. The sky hung heavy over the tattered roofs of beach houses. Wind pushed the odor of pluff mud and the departing rideshare back into the trees.

"You have to come home." Her uncle's voice had been flat on the phone the day before. She hadn't spoken to him in years, and nearly hung up before he said, "The house is in bad shape, so someone has to figure out what needs to be done. She left it to you, God knows why—"

"She what?" Lee interrupted.

"And I think it's high time you took some responsibility," he continued as though she hadn't said anything. As though she were a teenager who ran away to sleep on someone's couch instead of a woman who'd made a life for herself in Charleston.

"If it's that bad, I may as well just sell it," she'd retorted, stung.

"You can't just get rid of it! That house has weathered more than one hurricane. You need to do your duty, now."

Lee's sneakers ground into the wet, packed surface as she

strode down Palmetto. Most of the elevated houses in the first row had been red tagged, placards mounted along the stairs up to the front doors showing the building wasn't fit for habitation. A few sat despondent on the sand like toddlers whose legs had given out, windows weeping broken glass. Even the second-row houses had a fair number of reds, the rest bearing the yellow tag indicating moderate damage. Branches and heavy trash were pushed along the edge of where the road should have been.

Why was it so quiet? Lee expected someone would be outside, but there wasn't even a gull for company. The surf shoved at a mattress on the shore.

The house—her house, she supposed with a disquieting lurch—still had all of its posts elevating the structure, but at least a third of the siding was gone. All the shutters had been plucked away by the wind or the water, leaving the front exposed.

It had no card of any color. Lee peered at the houses on either side, both red tagged. Well, she'd be careful. She'd come all this way to diligently assess the property. Lee gave the stairs a push just in case, but they seemed stable enough. She dug the familiar key out of her coat and let herself in.

Lack of shutters didn't combat the gloom of the sky. Lee paused at the threshold, waiting for her eyes to adjust. Her nose didn't need any time, and she covered it against the rot. Gingerly stepping from the entry into the living room, she picked her path over the remains of window frames and kitchen chairs.

The couch sprawled across the room hadn't let go of its water, heavy cushions near bursting. Despite the wetness, they were thick with growth—a gray-green furriness that definitely wasn't the color she remembered. The bolsters were starting to split at the corners, little tears showing the sodden stuffing within. Milky light from the sole remaining window caught the hair-like extensions of something yellow and fungal colonizing part of one wall. All the furniture had been jumbled and broken, expanding to fill the space.

Lee coughed lightly, trying to expel the fetid air pressing against her. More than just the couch was decaying in this room, but she couldn't immediately see the cause. Perhaps fish had been carried in by the hurricane, left here to gasp and heave their last.

Was anything worth salvaging? The linoleum underfoot had swollen unevenly, and Lee took tiny steps toward the center of the room. The flood line ran above waist height.

She had written off the entire contents when she looked toward the bedroom in the back. From this angle, light caught an unbroken pane of glass in a picture frame on the wall.

Her mother had cherished that photo: Lee's grandmother standing, grim as Sundays, carrying Lee's mother in what was probably a christening dress. She stared at the camera in a way that had always struck Lee as quietly furious.

The water line ran just underneath the picture frame. How it hadn't been knocked off the wall when everything else in the house had been tumbled merrily about, Lee didn't know, but there it was—her mother's favorite picture.

Christ. She had to go get it, didn't she? Proof she'd been a good girl, that she'd gone to the house, and that she could be trusted to make the smart choice about what to do next.

Much of the debris and boards tangled across the back of the room had their nails turned obligingly upward, and Lee had to move carefully to get through. She was so focused on the terrain that she didn't see the rotting corpse on the far side of the couch until she was nearly on top of it.

Crayfish would eat anything, and two of them crawled over the torn belly of the stingray. Strands of sea grass twined around it, and bugs scurried out of sight underneath. The wings were folded like arms. It looked half alive with the movement of scavengers growing fat off the body. Lee's sense of smell seemed to intensify until the stink was intolerable.

She just had to step past it. She'd made her way to Charleston and started an entire damn career in food—made her way from dishes to being a line cook, and you didn't do that by being unable to cope with chaos and a whole mess of gross tasks. She exhaled.

The floor squelched, giving slightly underfoot as she touched the picture. Lee clamped her hand around the frame and turned back to the living room.

The sea skate's skin distended as though something moved inside it, and Lee's breath fled first her lungs and then the house.

It was just the carrion eaters, she thought, just another dead fish. No threat.

The belly raised and lowered, and then the body rolled over. Between one moment and the next, the wings narrowed into arms, a familiar vaccination scar near the shoulder. A human head emerged from the mangled skin. It stared up at her, clouded eyes running with dislodged burrowing creatures. It freed one limb from under the waterlogged couch and placed the bloated hand on the floor as though to get up.

When its mouth opened, Lee gulped for air to scream. It said, "We named you after her, you know."

It laid a soft hand across Lee's shoe before she could bolt, sighing "Stay…"

Lee felt the word and the wetness soak through her sneaker and sock, binding her to the floor. The damp clamminess spread along the top and sides of her foot, filming over her fear with a dull passivity. Dimly, dreamily, she could feel that prickling growth sneaking higher. As part of her brain emitted the high warning peal of terror, the moisture furred around her ankle and then her calf. She could feel the taint swirling in her blood like tendrils of milk rising in tea. The creature crawled closer, looping the fingers of its free hand around Lee's other ankle.

"Pretty as a peach, just like you," it whispered. "She did her duty by the family. Bore her responsibility with honor. You'll do your duty, won't you, Lee?"

Do your duty. Lee heard her uncle's sour voice again, remembered his shadow in her door. How her mother told her to hush, she must have misunderstood. Lee's nerves sparked raw with combined horror and rage, stifled under the thing's seeping influence.

From the front of the house, there came a creak. It distracted her from the wet stroke creeping above her knees. She drew in a ragged breath.

"Is anyone in here?" The firm, annoyed, blessedly human voice from the door may as well have come with a glowing exit sign.

The sound shattered Lee's compliance—she had to get out. In one sharp movement, she kicked free of the grasping fingers, recoiling until her back hit the wall. She spared one glance for the kitchen, utterly blocked by the pile of cabinetry and appliances, and then out the shattered back window. Debris filled the beach below—it would be madness to try to jump clear. Her heart tried to lurch free of her chest.

The thing peered up at her, lips parting to speak her name, a trap she wouldn't escape again.

"Pretty as a peach, just like you," it whispered.

Lee lunged toward the other voice, leaping over the glistening form on the floor.

She put one foot on the arm of the couch. It sank into the soft fabric as she pushed off again, and she thudded down into the slimy embrace of mold and sea water and polyester. Her momentum carried her forward toward the other arm, and she crashed into it only to slide onto the floor.

Something thumped softly behind her, and Lee staggered to her feet. Grey light fell in from the entryway and she went that way with little heed for the obstacles in between, clattering and kicking a path. A woman in a dark uniform and fluorescent vest leaned into the room, flashlight increasing the thin illumination.

"What in the—" the police officer began, but then Lee barreled into the door frame beside her.

"Run," she gasped. She could feel the ooze clinging to her cheek and throat, the rot covering her swelling ankles. Her coat and pants clung to her. The police officer stepped back, and Lee hurled herself down until she'd made it to the sand.

The woman's hand manacled around Lee's arm as she sucked in breath after breath, staring at the empty doorway. The sky leaned over them both.

"No one is supposed to go inside a red-tagged structure!" the cop shouted at her. "What were you thinking? Is that worth whatever tetanus bullshit you've just given yourself?"

Nothing moved except Lee's chest and the wind. Her hand started to cramp, and she realized she was still holding the photo. Lee's grandmother glared up at her. A smeary yellow drop landed on the glass, and Lee wiped it away by reflex.

A car crunched to a stop down by the Bi-Lo, and Lee straightened. "You're right, I shouldn't have done it. Stupid."

The cop let go of Lee's arm. "You should be glad someone saw you go in there and called." After a moment, the police officer asked, "What the hell'd you see, get you out so fast?"

Lee rasped out a laugh, wiping a wet thumb over the glass again. "Whole lot of bad history, water damage, and whatever I'm wearing," she said. "I'm not going in there again. I'll get a company to come take care of this."

"First you need to go get yourself checked out," the other woman said. After a moment, she asked, "You have a car, or are you going to get that crap all over mine?" She made Lee stay there while she relocked the door.

On the way to the urgent care, Lee cracked the window. The smell of the salt marsh rolled over her, rich and fertile, as the Mystery Tree swept by outside.

"You know you're lucky you got out of there in one piece," the cop said.

"There are a lot of different kinds of strength," Lee replied, meeting her grandmother's gaze through glass. "But I come from a resilient line."

SILVER HANDS AGAINST THE DEVIL

by JESSICA LÉVAI

I've met the Devil three times.

I grew up outside one of the walled enclaves where the rich hid with their technology once the world's farmlands turned into deserts and its cities became swamps. You were born and spent your entire life behind the walls, so you were never supposed to see what powers had flowed in to claim what your ancestors left behind. I heard rumors of fierce monsters roaming the wastes and personally saw a neighbor transformed into something more like a frog than a man. And the first time I met the Devil, it was because my father had traded me to him for the promise of gold.

My father wasn't like your mother. He was poor and desperate, but I didn't believe he would do it. Even right before the axe came down, I didn't think I could mean so little to him that he would give the Devil what he wanted. I was wrong. It turns out that even without my hands, I was too clean for the Devil to touch, so I got away that time. From the Devil and my father, both. After my husband made me my first pair of silver hands, I convinced myself that my father was an anomaly. That the world had made him too small to love properly. Maybe if our situation had been different, the Devil wouldn't have come anywhere near us.

"Even without my hands, I was too clean for the Devil to touch."

Of course, that isn't true. I had an inkling when your mother called me and told me about your problem. Madeleine was an old friend of my husband's. She never liked me much, born on the outside as I was, but she knew my story and hoped that I could help her, and you. I was certainly going to try. She wasn't like my father, and I thought that made her better. After all, she wasn't looking for gold. She had only made the deal because she was so desperate to have a child.

After she told me your story, I met the Devil for the second time. I was in the hardware store, putting jugs of lye into my cart, when I heard a hissing sound. Not just the lights over the aisle, not just the servos in my hands, but a sort of sound he makes just by moving through the air. You've heard it, so you understand what I mean. I don't think I have to make you promise me that if you hear it again, you run.

He followed me as I left the cleaning supplies and made my way to the power tools. When it became clear I wasn't going to speak first, he said, "I hear you were visiting our mutual friends Madeleine LaGrange and her lovely family," he said. "Did she mention me?"

I sighed and picked up a cordless drill. "I don't see that you have any power here, Nick. Your deal with her is long over."

"Is that what she told you? Two roses, and she was only supposed to eat one. Greedy minx ate both. That was against the rules. Hence her...difficult childbirth."

I told you about some of the stuff I've seen outside the walls. But I swear, when your mother told me about when you and your brother were born, I got chills. Maybe it's because I'm a mother myself, and the thought of something legless and scaly coming out of someone is too much, even if it's followed by a normal, healthy baby. I told him, "I think you've gotten your money's worth on that joke."

He chuckled darkly. "Yes, that was funny. But she still owes me, or I wouldn't be here." The Devil counted on his fingers, "I told her I would claim one of her children. She never asked me which one, until it was too late. When I sent her serpent son back to her to demand a bride, she knew there was only one girl who would satisfy me."

I thought of you, so alone and so scared, only a little older than I was when I lost my hands. "Bethany is an innocent."

"So were you," he spat back at me. "I guess I like a challenge." My fingers shook inside my gloves, and I nearly dropped the drill into my cart. I squeezed the button on its handle, felt it whirr to life, the noise drowning out his hiss for a little while. The Devil brushed his finger over the calfskin of my gloves and they started to melt, like he'd breathed acid on them. The gloves went up like steam and my hands, my silver robot hands, sparkled in the fluorescent light. "Still my favorite metal," he said. "You know, I heard a rumor that your flesh hands had grown back."

"Don't believe everything you hear," I said.

"At least you have a souvenir of me," he said.

"I have a souvenir of my husband." I wrenched my cart away from him.

I was ready to storm off, but his voice has a way of holding someone, even me. "I wasn't finished. Your friend hasn't given you a full account of her feeble attempts to pay what she owes." He filled in all the blanks.

Finally, he was finished. "Get behind me," I said, shoving the cart to the checkout.

***

You and I both know how much your mother loved you, right? At the time, I didn't, though I've seen the proof now. Then, I swear, my father's axe flashed in front of my eyes, over and over again, as I screamed at Maddy. "How could you do such a thing?"

She'd lost the bluster from our earlier meeting, when she talked to me like I was some new hire. Now she was shrunken, quiet. "That thing demanded a bride. I wasn't going to give him Bethany. But there are always girls on the outside, girls who will risk anything to join a family in a walled city."

"And girls outside the wall don't matter, do they?" My hands clenched, risking the delicate machinery, the gears my son had so carefully arranged when he last upgraded them. "How many, Maddy? How many did you give him?"

She swallowed. "Three."

I couldn't speak. I wanted to scream, but no sound came out. I covered my face with my hands and focused on the feel of the cool metal against my skin.

After a while Maddy said, "Are you still going to help me?"

"Why should I?" I said between my fingers. That's the thing

about meeting the Devil: those encounters tend to sharpen your faith in people, and not always in the right way. "You gave the Devil what he wanted." She started to interrupt me, but I held a silver finger in her face and she shut her mouth. "So I don't have a lot of sympathy for you. But I said I'd help, and I will."

***

You were there the third time I met the Devil.

I didn't know what to expect from you. You learned your lines. You didn't complain when I layered you in every dress you own. You didn't freak out when I told you what the lye was for. But I was worried that you would panic, or give up, and that's just another thing I was wrong about. I'm sorry about that, just like I'm a little sorry I didn't trust your mother.

Madeleine and I had just enough time to get out of your room and position ourselves by the spy holes when the serpent, her son and your brother, slithered in through the window. And God, I wasn't ready. Ten feet long if he was an inch, covered with slick, glittering, silver scales. He looked too shiny, almost robotic. His voice was like nothing I ever heard, except it wasn't. It was the Devil's voice the whole time.

"Take off your dress," I heard him hiss at you. I didn't hear you answer. I strained my ears and I willed you to talk, but I could barely see you through the hole. I figured you were frozen, terrified.

I was swearing, your mother looking at me like I was going to get everyone killed, and then I heard it, so soft, you said, "Take off a skin." I heard this dry, rustling noise, only it wasn't the Devil hissing, and when I looked back through the hole, there was a snakeskin on top of the first dress. And each time he asked you to strip, you told him to shed. Your voice got stronger and stronger. I looked at your mother and saw that she was so proud of you. You should know that. I was proud, too. I thought it was going to work. A few more layers, and you could use the lye to burn and banish the monster forever. There's no way he would have survived.

But the Devil, as they say, is in the details. And as the serpent shed skins, he grew weaker, slimier, more repulsive. But you knew that your brother was in there, way before I did and a second before your mother. You were trying to talk to him, but you didn't even have a name to use. We are going to have to fix that, soon.

I decided I was going to have to go in and end the monster myself, when suddenly I was knocked over by Madeleine. She left her spy hole and pushed me aside so I fell. I twisted my ankle, and you can still hear the broken servo buzzing in my right hand. I could only scream at her to stop, but then, of course, it was too late.

I dragged myself into the room enough to see it all. Madeleine threw herself on the serpent and pulled you free as it was trying to squeeze you to death in its coils. Then she took that writhing mass in her arms, blood and goo oozing everywhere. It slashed at her with its teeth, but she held it and wouldn't let go.

When she screamed, "No! Take me! You've tortured my children long enough!" I was sure we were all going to die. The lights in the room all popped at the same time, shooting sparks everywhere, refracting against the scales and my hands. When I found my flashlight and scanned the room, Maddy was gone. So was the serpent. There was only you, and the young man next to you, who looked like you, hanging on for dear life.

***

So that's the story of the three times I met the Devil, which is three times more than anyone should. I really hope he leaves the both of you alone going forward. If he doesn't, remember how much your mother loved you. How much you love each other. Love is never a sure thing in this world, but it's the only thing that'll keep him off your back.

You don't have to come back with me to my city. I can drop you anywhere you like. But I need to go home, see my husband and my kids and my grandkids. Maybe one of them can fix my hand. It'll be harder to hug them if it's broken.

A HOUSE WITHOUT GHOSTS

by M. LOPES DA SILVA

Our new house is not haunted.

It is a beautiful house; excessively beautiful. The type of ideal object I am accustomed to looking at sideways through digital tours and magazine photo spreads. My body is too solid to move through these light halls. My hands are too oily to risk touching something and leaving behind fingerprints. My footsteps echo too loudly; I shouldn't have worn my shoes inside.

***

"It's too expensive for ghosts," my husband jokes when the real estate agent tells us that the previous residents had died there.

"How did they die?" I ask—too morbid. My husband immediately fills the bright, empty space with a laugh.

The real estate agent has an answer ready (she had everything ready: the house full of books unread since the 1950s but bought for their gilded spines that catch the light and twinkle like jewelry). "Natural causes. They were a sweet elderly couple. The neighbors loved them."

The neighbors are not nearby. I wonder what they loved about them.

***

There is no trace of the people that used to live here. I can't find a single scuff on the hardwood flooring or the mildest of dents by the staircase. Everything is so clean. The paint is a glaring white that bounces the natural light around and around like a rubber ball. The glass in all the windows is thick, lens-like. Everything is magnified inside the house. If there were any ghosts around, we certainly would have seen them.

***

People leave behind pieces of themselves: stains and smears and garbage. They carve initials. They wear down paving stones. They forge wish-paths through carefully planted gardens.

There is nothing like people in this house. There's only us. My husband is meticulous, erasing every trace of himself as he moves along. He is the one that picks up the plates and knows every chemical counterspell to a stain. I am the mess; stumbling, forgetting. But even my messes seem small here. They are swallowed up by white space. There's no reason to hire a maid.

At night when my husband stays late at the office and the sky-lights drag in the stars there is only one heart beating in my bed, too loudly.

***

Our closest neighbor is another house so well-hedged that I can't be certain of its style or size. There's a brick buzz box just out-side, and two men stand nearby vaping and leaning against a dirty car hood.

"What kind of car?" My husband asks later, but it was one of those shapeless cars without anything for my memory to hold onto.

"An anything car," I say. "It doesn't matter."

But he frowns deeply: this point matters to *him*.

"A black car, maybe gray," I offer. He looks disgusted.

"What did they want?"

"To take pictures," I say, but I've lost the point already. I sur-render unhappily. "They were paparazzi."

His eyes light up. "So our neighbors are movie stars, huh? We'll never see them unless they drive a sports car into our pool."

He sounds satisfied—gleeful. The mental image of someone in the green lozenge of our pool, fighting a car door and the water and their own inebriation, fills me with anxiety. I can't smile. Or I won't.

***

We are at a dinner party when I realize that I have forgotten what I studied in college. I stare straight ahead, trying to recollect a single class I've taken that wasn't one of the general requisites. I'm blank. Nothing comes to me. I turn to my husband and prompt him: "Weren't you always picking me up after that one class I was taking?"

"Yeah," he says brightly. "The traffic was hell at that hour and I could never find parking. Would you pass the salt?"

I pass the salt. I laugh, and hate the nervous sound I make. I can't remember when I stopped hanging out at friends' places and started going to dinner parties. The dress I am wearing feels too tight. When I bring it up to my husband later that evening he mentions bloating and asks if my period is about to start. Do I know the date of my last menstrual cycle?

I don't. The dates in my calendar book have all been left empty for months now. He clucks his tongue at me.

"It just seems to me that if you have something recurring like a menstrual cycle you should know more about it," he says.

"It's irregular. It's always been irregular," I reply, then a little braver: "You want to know the unknowable."

His eyes are so sharp he doesn't need a cutting retort. I wither, and offer the last Tuesday of the previous month, maybe.

***

Alone, my hands drift along the sides of my torso: crawling, teasing. There is no need to shorten the hunt. There can only be the hunt; the hunting, if I like. My fingers interlace with intangibles. I press the button on my clitoral stopwatch, and suddenly I can control time. I can rewind. I can fast forward. I can sit forever paused in one long moment for minutes or hours or days if I want to.

Did they die in this bedroom, holding each other? Or did they choose one of the other, larger bedrooms that face the cliffs instead of the sea? Did they have time to choose? I want to know. Does my body overlap the space that their corpses inhabited? A vague image of entwined arms like a heraldic crest creeps across my mental eye—was it really natural causes, or something more sinister like murder—or suicide? Or—? Or just one life ending and another life clinging onto the husk of the first until their time ebbed out. I sigh. The perverse tangle of life and death threads through me like roots. When I cum, my orgasm's ripple leaves a soft ringing in my ear that I cannot explain.

***

"There should be ghosts," I say, much later. We look at the ocean together through the giant glass wall of our living room in silence. The sound of the sea is swallowed up at our distance. It's like an animated picture of an ocean; a pretty fantasy.

"Ghosts are not an amenity," my husband chides me. "Why do you want them so badly? I don't want any." He wants to play. His breath is red like wine at my neck.

I cannot be playful. My lips won't rubber up at the edges. I can't think of a decent joke to reply with.

"It's like they vanished without a trace. Two people—two whole people!"

"People vanish all the time. It's Los Angeles," he says. "Half the time you move here and realize you can't afford it."

I was born in Los Angeles; my husband moved here, from another city in another state. I've never been able to make the kind of money that he does easily. I have never been able to pay the rent without the minimum of one roommate. I have never owned before.

"That's the difference between us," I say, "you have experience with owning things."

He tilts his head, regarding me. "I do."

When he sinks his fingers into the flesh of my arms (so soft, my muscles pliant, too claylike for proper Hollywood) I open my mouth. Then I'm tasting his tongue tasting me, twisting.

We are alone. There is no chill from beyond puckering my skin. The dead are not watching us. They cannot. The walls are still bare, still glaring white; we cannot agree on anything to hang up on them. I squeeze my eyes shut and stumble to the bedroom with him.

When we are in bed we make the discovery that his left nipple is missing.

He is embarrassed—almost apologetic. That nipple has never proved to be unreliable before. He makes a joke about leaving it behind at the office and when I start to panic he holds me and hushes me and says he will make an appointment to see a dermatologist in the morning.

"Don't get so upset—shouldn't you be comforting me?" he asks.

And I feel so ashamed that I sit up and try to hold him but the position is awkward so we both end up laughing. I'd missed this easy feeling; where had we been hiding it?

***

I wake up and reach for my phone (I don't reach for him; I know that he's already gone). I want to look at old pictures of us. We only have a few: he doesn't like having his picture taken. I recollect a shining two-shot of our faces beaming over drinks with fruit clinging to the rims of our glasses (pineapples or oranges? or some other citrus?) and I want to see what bar we were tagged in. I remember pieces of that night: getting drunk and howling karaoke to a benignly disinterested crowd. I'd discussed the history of karaoke passionately. He'd tucked a curl of my hair behind one of my ears, and told me how he'd been thinking about buying a house in town sometime soon.

I thumb the screen and it remains dark. Smeary-eyed, I sit up and grope for the phone charger on my nightstand. I plug in my phone and wait. It can't be too late but the light is already dazzlingly bright in the house. I squint and focus on the black rectangle of the electronic device in front of me, waiting for the reassuring icon of a charging battery to pop up there.

I spend a long time waiting before I give up and take it to a repair shop.

***

My period isn't coming. I buy a pregnancy test at a drug store, then seclude myself in the narrow bathroom there. I pee on a stick, then lean against a stack of cardboard boxes advertising enemas as I wait for the test to report back on the current state of my womb: no occupancy.

I should be relieved, but I am still worried—maybe more worried than I was before. My missing blood troubles me.

***

"She thinks it might be hormones," he tells me.

"What?"

My husband stares at me. "The dermatologist? She thinks it might be hormones."

"Oh," I say. He's taking off his jacket and loosening his tie. "But you aren't taking any hormones."

He shrugs. "Maybe it's something from all the meat I've been eating. Apparently, this has never happened before, so she's only theorizing, but I guess this gives us a reason to finally go vegetarian like you've always wanted. Maybe you can pick something up at the farmer's market this weekend."

"That's it? She just wants you to give up meat?"

"She ran some tests and wants me to come back, but so far, yes. I thought you'd be relieved."

"I don't know." I frown. "Aren't you worried that she doesn't really know what's wrong?"

"But she thinks it's probably hormones. Fine. What's the point in worrying about it?" His eyes are bright; brighter than the dimming sunlight caught on the walls and sealed under glass. I squint.

"Are you all right? You look like you have one of your headaches again. Maybe you should see the doctor."

***

Maybe I should see the doctor, but instead I go see my friend, Rebecca. She's not my closest friend, in fact she's more of my husband's friend than my own, but she's the first one that gets back to me when I reach out online. We meet at a pop-up restaurant wedged into the wealth of Santa Monica. The theme of the restaurant eludes me; there are pink drapes and framed photographs of lone cacti on the walls. There is an anony-gramness to the place. I order a poem that seems to imply pancakes on the menu, but when it arrives it is more of a soggy omelette. Rebecca takes pictures of the food while I talk about the new house.

"Why would your real estate agent even tell you that?" She asks me.

"Doesn't she have to?"

Rebecca turns her saucer of gelée a few degrees clockwise, then takes a picture.

"Not unless there was a violent crime or something. Natural causes? No need to tell you about it in the state of California."

I stare at Rebecca blankly. "That's odd."

"Very. Do you still have her number?"

Of course I don't.

***

My cloud data didn't update with my photographs before my phone died, and the repair people tell me that my SIM card was 'wiped clean' somehow, so in my car I pick up the phone and shut my eyes and try to remember what it felt like—that night and being in love—and when nothing comes to me I shake and squeeze the phone so tightly that the screen cracks a little and I finally feel something terrible. Monstrous. I can't bring myself to go back inside the repair shop. I decide to buy a new phone, instead.

***

He wants me to make dinner every night. He wants me to settle in. At the house I never feel "at home", even though I keep trying to domesticate this space. I buy a vibrant rug and a yellow vase for the living room, but the rug is stained and gone to the dry cleaners within a day, and the flowers I put in the vase keep dying. He throws them out. The empty slim yellow vessel is less than yolk in all the eggy whiteness. There is only the rubber ball of light, bouncing around and around. I can't remember my great-grandmother's recipe for feijoada in this place. But I'm not supposed to make meat; I will have to cook something else. I will have to improvise. I pick up the kitchen knife.

***

I remember pieces, chopped up.

I was a suitcase child, grown into a suitcase woman, who was definitely going somewhere when she met someone who'd made her forget she'd ever had a destination.

Someone who thought he might buy a house in town. A brand new house, one that couldn't possibly be haunted. A white plaster box on a cliff overlooking the sea. My name wasn't even on the paperwork.

It was never really my house, only his.

***

"Put down the knife," he says, "you look ridiculous."

I begin to cry. "Why can't you take this seriously? Please, just listen to me!"

"I'm listening," he says. "I'm listening right now, aren't I? So?"

"So." I take a deep breath. "You never liked that night at the karaoke bar—you hated the way it made you feel!"

"Right." My husband's features are stuck in that ugly, graceless place in between amusement and anger. "It was a very awkward evening. I don't like singing karaoke—is that what this is about?"

I grit my teeth: nothing was coming out in the right order. Why did everything sound so incredibly irrational right now? But then, of course, I knew the answer.

"You don't like facing yourself. You don't like being vulnerable," I say. And there is a hush in the house deeper than the absence of sound; this is a listening hush. Things older than concrete and plaster long-poured into the bones of this house are waiting for me to speak.

"What I'm saying is that this is…this house erases things. Things that you don't want or like anymore. It's your house, so it's listening to you."

He laughs: I've surprised him. "Are you saying that I didn't like my own nipple enough?"

I wait, staring at him, unwilling to put down the knife.

"Well, maybe you're right about that. That one always looked sort of funny to me." He says something else, but low enough that I can't hear it.

"What do you like about me?" I ask suddenly.

"Oh, is this what it's really all about?"

"You like my body, right? And how 'sexual' I am?"

*There is only a wet, sealed hollow of bone and meat,
fused as if there'd never been a mouth there in the first place.*

He snorts a little. "You've got a funny way of getting me to call you 'sexy'."

"But you don't like it when I get my period. And you didn't like my major in college. And you must hate my family—where are they? Same thing with my friends. You don't like ghosts so there aren't any ghosts. There isn't even a gory backstory to keep you awake at night. This place is haunted by *you*."

My husband stares at my mouth for such a long period of time that I raise my fingers protectively to hide it from him.

"What is it? What are you going to do?" I ask.

He shakes his head. "Sometimes I don't know if it's better or worse this way."

"What?"

"Oh, it's too complicated. Nothing I guess."

"You can't say something like that and just leave it. Tell me what's wrong."

He studies me. "I hate listening to you when you're scared like this, but you have such a pretty voice," he says finally.

The living room is so still, so absolutely quiet that I want to scream. I want to smash the silence and smear snot and blood on the walls. I want to tear the plaster apart with my teeth.

But my mouth is gone now—my lips and tongue and teeth altogether vanished. There is only a wet, sealed hollow of bone and meat, fused as if there'd never been a mouth there in the first place.

I drop the knife. When I look up my husband is no longer there.

He'd never liked himself very much.

***

I feel calm now; my fear is gone. I have a clear mental picture—I won't have it for very long.

The house is clean, the paint so white and new that it doesn't need a fresh coat. My husband does not need to pick up after anyone any more. The ocean's roar is still politely muted by the glass; two whole people aren't nearly as noisy as the entire Pacific Ocean.

The light is so dazzling that I cannot tell if the sign on our lawn has the name of a politician or a real estate agent on it.

We won't be in.

THE REACHING SEA

by VICTORIA NATIONS

Mom didn't like Barry to touch the hands that washed up, so he stopped telling her about them. If she knew how often he saw them, she might tell him he couldn't visit the beach at all, and he didn't know what he'd do if he couldn't look out at the water.

He and his mom surf fished every day. She called it a break from his studies, but the beach didn't stop her instruction of him, her constant vigilance and comments. Since he'd turned thirteen, he called her Mary in his head. It put them on equal footing. He was grateful when their steps crunched on the boards, though only the barest sheen of ice formed on the pier. The mist was too salty, and everything close to the water felt gummy with it.

Mary stalked down the beach, her hair tucked in a sweater cap, as controlled and androgynous as the thick field coat she wore. She only looked at the water in passing, focusing on the way before them, down the beach to a good fishing spot. He trailed further and further back from her once they hit the sand, and his eyes scanned the waves.

The hands were never on the high tide line, never washed in at night for them to find in the morning. They always bobbed up as he was watching, tumbling in the waves, stiff and bloated. They landed where he could reach them, behind Mary's back.

It wasn't like they were gooey or bloody. It was so cold it was like picking up popsicles. They melted like popsicles, too, if he held them for long. He thought about bringing a napkin to wrap around them, like Mary used to do with his ice cream cone, but she'd notice if he had a wad of napkins in his coat. So he slipped the hands in his pocket, instead. Never more than one a day. He blamed his wet pants on the splashing waves.

He kicked at the sand, relishing the slopping sound and splash as a clod dropped into a wave. The hand slipped into his pocket soundlessly. He'd look at it closer when he got home and tucked it away with the others.

***

That child, Mary thought. *He's...* Her evaluation unraveled there. Barry was changing so fast, and she couldn't tell where his thoughts were anymore. He'd taken to wearing baggy pants, then spent their walk tugging them up. The December wind beat at them, making them cling to his slender legs. White-blond hair whipped around his face, and his dark blue eyes tracked the outgoing surf wetting the sand and pulling out, wetting it less each time. He'd walk into her if she stopped. His eyes were restless, never staying in one spot, missing the saltwater seeping into his shoes as he shuffled along. He was watching for the trash that washed up on the beach. Obsessed.

Focus was good in a boy. It was rare for his age, she knew. She'd always been dismayed by the empty heads of the locals. They wandered in the waves, too, eyes drained of color, skin pruned with water. They brought home all manner of distractions and never accomplished anything. The sea captured each and every one of them.

She'd made sure her boy was disciplined, fishing until dinner was caught, then helping to transform it into a proper meal at home. Barry would leave this place with skills, unlike the haphazard townies who pulled in nets and ate the same slop of creatures they sold for cat food and chum.

He was too thin, perhaps. It was the growth spurt. He'd shot up tall, his limbs suddenly long and covered in downy light hair. His navy eyes shone with intelligence, never lightening like the locals, but his focus was more and more on the relentless sea, sweeping back and forth. He barely looked at her while they fished now.

"Barry."

The boy trailed behind her, his feet plodding through the sand, wet impression after wet impression. Sand stuck to his shoes and pants legs now, and clumps of it swung with each step.

"Barry." She spoke louder, and the sharpness caught his attention. He turned his head, swiveling so it faced mostly towards her. His eyes were faraway, his thoughts still on something else. One hand tugged his pants up again. The other stayed sunk into his pants pocket.

"You're wet. Are you cold?" She wanted to know so much more. *What are you thinking? What are you planning to do?*

"No, Mom." The hand slid from his pocket and he wiped it on his pants. The sandy hand was a tell. She'd told him many times before, and he just wasn't learning this one lesson.

He never dropped his eyes, though. He'd learned that. She'd told him that the person who dropped their eyes lost the conversation. He'd never dropped his eyes from her ever again, a strength of will that was disconcerting and made her proud.

***

Barry hadn't brought the first hand home. He'd tried. He'd wanted to very much. But his mom kept way too close an eye on him when he was younger.

"Barry, put that down." Her voice had rung out, louder than the wind coming off the water. Barry had waded calf-deep to catch the thing floating towards him. He'd just realized he was holding a human hand. *A hand! So weird!* And she was there, insisting he give it up.

"Mom, look! It used to be alive." Barry cringed, remembering how he'd tried to explain it to her, but the excitement tangled his tongue. He needed to convey how important a discovery it was. Mom wasn't moved by his enthusiasm, though.

"That tells me it's rotten now. Drop it."

No investigation. She hadn't even seemed surprised. She just made him drop the first hand into the wet sand and keep walking. It had landed with a squelch. Barry kept looking back, waiting to see what it would do, and it was gone when the next wave covered it.

"Come on," his mom had said, and he had, running to catch up with her even though her back was turned. He'd thought about pleading with her to wait. He'd thought about running back to find the hand. But he hadn't. He'd followed, as she expected, even though his eyes kept dragging back to that patch of sand. He watched new waves tumble, thinking they'd reveal the hand again, but the beach was empty.

He'd been fretful for the rest of the walk. The hand had wanted him to find it. He could tell. His mom wanted him to focus, so he did. And he'd been looking for hands ever since.

***

Focusing didn't make more hands show up, though. And it didn't help him figure out what to do with a hand once the next one came.

He'd thought he was so slick. He'd stopped at the end of the pier, stood straight, and insisted to his mom that she let him fish by himself. He was a teenager now. She'd searched his face. She'd known, he was sure of it, known that he was hiding something. But she'd relented when he stared back at her.

Mary, he'd rehearsed, *I'm going to fish alone*. The adult name had made his mental voice shake. It must've shown, based on Mary's amused face. He'd finally breathed when she turned and headed down the beach.

His boldness paid off after weeks of searching the waves. A hand flopped over at his feet, and he'd nabbed it clumsily, jumping up as if Mary would appear. Wrinkled gray skin felt thick over its bony frame. The curved fingers poked against his body as he frantically dipped his hand, searching for the pocket opening, and shoved it inside after several tries.

Victory. Against what, he wasn't sure. But the presence of the hand felt like he'd scored something big.

Barry hid that first hand in the cellar, behind his grandmother's canning that Mary never used and never threw out. Even toweled off, it was spongy and rank, like the rind of a rotting fruit. The hand lay in a jar with punched holes in the top, like for a frog. Hands didn't breathe. He knew that. But he'd argued with himself about keeping it sealed or letting air get in to dry it out, and the holes won out. A week later, he wished he'd kept the lid intact. The hand grew tendrils, like sprouting potato eyes. The filaments were white and bulbous, and stunk like rotten eggs. Worse, sea lice got in the holes and scurried all over the chewed flesh. A drift of shed exoskeletons collected in the bottom of the jar.

He washed the pocked hand, scraping off the growth, and moved it to the old freezer with a reminder to not be so childish the next time.

***

"I taught you better."

Her son stared at her. A year ago, he would've been looking up at her, his lips quivering if she spoke sharply to him. A year from now, his stoicism may turn to arrogance, and she'd have to fix that when it came. But for now, her strong teenager stood before her without a shred of reaction. She worked to keep her face severe. The cellar smelled briny, like the sea was seeping through the walls.

"Barry, have you hidden something down here? Trash you picked up on the beach?"

Barry was quiet. Then he slowly swung his head up and down. His eyes stayed on hers as he nodded.

"They'll rot, you know." Mary zeroed in on a bundle of rags. The smell deepened when she knelt close to them. She parted the folded cloth, assuming something would drop out, but it was empty. Barry took the rags from her hand, his mouth set into a grim line.

What are you thinking? What are you hiding? He had something squirreled away. The nasty things would spoil him as truly as they would decay themselves.

"You think I'm controlling, keeping you from your trash." She met his stare. Barry didn't flinch. "But that's not why. I stop you because of the horrible things that happen."

"They aren't horrible." Barry's brow was bunched low over his eyes. Anger, frustration. Something was brewing there that aged him.

"I'm not talking about your… things. Whatever you're finding on the beach." Mary paused, wondering how to say it. He was older. He wasn't old enough. "It's this place."

"What about it?"

"Just, it sucks you in." *And you'll never leave, son. And you have to leave.* "Stay out of the water. Promise me."

Barry nodded again, but in his eyes, he answered. *You can't stop me.*

***

Mary's talk only made the hands seem more exciting. She was bonkers, of course. And she hated the town, the sea. All she talked about was him getting out of there. Barry took bleak joy in dragging her to the beach after that. He walked briskly to the pier, fishing gear swinging, then let her lead when they got to the sand. His gaze never swung landward now, to follow her. His eyes only tracked to the horizon and back, searching.

He didn't tell Mary, but he was pretty sure the sea noticed. Waves rolled in, cycling together to curl the entire length of the beach. White foam crept in and pulled out, a magician's gloved fingers revealing hidden things and making them disappear again.

Barry could feel his pulse syncing with them, his breath pulling in and out to the same tempo.

As if vying for his attention, the hands danced in the waves, hundreds of them on the horizon. They bobbed and waved in the water. Hands of all sizes. Thick and gnarled. Tiny and translucent. The pale winter sun glinted off their fingernails and the occasional ring. The more he watched them, the more animated they got. Fingers wiggled in spidery gestures. One leapt, popped up by a wave, and dove into the water like it was doing a crawl stroke, paddling towards him.

When the swimmer got to him and scrabbled onto the toe of his wet shoe, he scooped it up like a wriggling puppy and popped it into his pocket. He caressed it the whole way home.

***

More hands came, every day now, inching their way to shore. There were too many for Barry to put in his pockets, and the ones left behind crawled after him, dragging through the sand, rolling back into the water as if they couldn't survive in the air for long. At first, Barry was excited by their interest. He watched their tapping and waggling fingers intensely, sure they were communicating something to him.

All of the newer hands in the cellar wiggled their fingers. Barry tickled his against them, trying to talk back. They were still gray and waterlogged. Their knuckles bunched into fat folds when the fingers curled, the flesh loose and sodden. They stroked up the underside of his arm and climbed to his shoulder, tickling the back of his neck.

The movements made him shiver.

Fingers pushed into his mouth if he let the hands too close to his face. The first time it happened, Barry was repulsed by the shriveled flesh, rough against his lips. He spat, trying to force it to out. He was even more repulsed when his mouth watered for it after the finger drew back.

When the hands reached for him again, he let them. He sucked the cold thumb into his cheek, wrapping his tongue around it. Nails scraped against his teeth, pushing his jaw wider, and he bit down. His teeth worried the flesh until he cut down to the bone. Loose pieces of skin and muscle lay in his mouth, tasteless, the salt of the sea sucked out of them. Barry pulled the chewed fingers from his mouth, and they curled and uncurled slowly.

They clamored for him after that. The floor teemed with them. He told them he would leave them there and not return, and their rustling sounded like whispers. Promises. Threats.

***

"Barry!" His mom called to him as he bolted out the door, but he didn't stop. He ran to the beach, refusing to be there for another of Mary's searches. The hands rolling around the cellar would be there when she looked or they wouldn't, and who cared.

It was still cold, even though the pier was too warmed to hold ice. A wet hint of spring blew in with the breeze, and he could smell the dune greenery popping out. His hair swiped his cheeks. When had it gotten so long?

The waves sprung up in jagged humps, crashing and spurting foam as they rammed into each other. Hands writhed in the walls of the waves, their fingers jutting out to drag foamy streaks through them. Closer to shore, arms flipped over and over, flabby extensions of the grasping hands smacking against the wet sand.

A beefy forearm covered in black hair thudded and rolled, too heavy to be dislodged from where it was stuck.

Children's arms moved together, clapping their attached hands with muffled glee.

A delicate hand reached up, propped up on an unseen elbow, and held steady, despite the water rushing on either side of it. A pale hand, limber as if alive, beckoned to Barry. He couldn't take his eyes off it.

It was only a short walk to where the waves broke and spread into thin sheets crawling up the beach. The tide was in and high. Barry reached for the hand tipped in lavender-tinged fingernails. It rolled, repeated, pleading without sound that he come to it. Come to her.

Barry stood ankle deep, but she was further out than she'd first seemed. He took another step, bending to reach, trying to stay out of the water, knowing the sand would give way. There would be a shelf, and then the ground would slip deeper, Mary had said so. He reached out, extending his arm as far as it would go, and her hand rolled on its wrist, motioning for him to come deeper.

The vice grip around his ankle clenched fast and tight, and it shocked a cry out of Barry. One moment the shushing rush of water ran past his skin, pushing his soaked sock around and filling the gaps in his shoe. The next, the wet fabric was ground against his skin, and his ankle bone seemed to squeak from the pressure. Barry stumbled and fell, everything in his body loose and unstable except for the foot planted in the sand, held there by the grip. A wave crashed close to him and seawater poured up the beach as he fell, drenching everything and spraying into his face.

Barry kicked his other foot against the hairy fingers wrapped around his ankle, a different thing than what had beckoned him. The forearm was nearly as thick as his leg, the muscles bunched as they held on tight. Panting, he kicked again, dislodging each finger, until the heavy hand finally fell off and lay there as if exhausted, the incoming water streaming between its upturned fingers. Barry crab walked back through the damp sand until he got above the tide line. Sand covered and clung to his wet clothes. He swiped gritty hands across eyes and peered across the waves.

The delicate hand in the waves was gone. The burly arm was buried or washed away. The sand below him was empty. All of the waves were empty, or the hands had withdrawn, sunk to where he couldn't see them. Barry thought the last must be true. They were there, waiting to snag him, waiting to hold him to the beach or drag him under.

***

Don't tell him you told him so. He might still be hiding. He might still be planning. Mary stood at the end of the pier, trying to keep from crying. Barry lay battered, but free, below her.

"Are you ok?" Mary asked, and Barry turned and squinted at her. His face was blanched, with barely any color except for spots on the apples of his cheek. His fair hair hung in his eyes, but she could still see his forehead. He was developing his first lines there. She should be angry. At his insolence. At his deception. But the way his eyes rolled around was pathetic. He so rarely needed her anymore, but he needed her now. There was still a chance.

She knelt beside him and helped him stand. Best they get back to higher ground.

"Do you see now?"

Barry gaped. Tears were starting, and he wasn't trying to stop them.

"This place. People get stuck here. It takes hold. Possesses you. But you don't have to stay."

Barry shook his head, but Mary couldn't tell if it was a nod or if a chill had wracked his body.

***

Mary glanced at her son, quick so he wouldn't notice while he stared over the water. He was fishing close to her today, the first time in a year. But not too close. The independence was still there. The focus. He understood more now. Maybe he would make better choices. Maybe he would tell her if he got into trouble again, before it got so out of hand.

Maybe. Probably not.

He squinted in the pale sun bouncing off the sea. It was choppy, and diffuse light lit everything with a soft glow. They hardly had shadows. But the sun still bothered him. With those washed-out eyes, he'd barely be able to open them in the full sunshine of summer. He could easily lose his way when it glittered off the water.

Mary pulled in her line to re-bait her hook and tossed it back out into the waves. Barry did the same, and a trick of light made it seem like a tiny hand caught it, but it probably just plunked down in a splash that looked that way.

AFTER THE APPLES

by BRIANA UNA McGUCKIN

Antiphony did not remember her father's face, but she recognized him in her mother's scars. The rows of tilled tissue on her mother's hind-legs reminded Antiphony of the farmer's fields, and when she was very young, she wondered whether there were seeds to sow for fur, so that her mother's coat might be restored.

"That's nothing, kitto," Widow Wit soothed as her daughter's damp nose traced the wounds. "He didn't get his teeth in, and the apples do for the pain."

On this and every night, Antiphony nodded but could not meet her mother's eyes. She did not like the apples. She would never say this aloud and despised herself for thinking it, because her mother was in pain. Finding the apples fermenting on the edge of the farmer's place had been a blessing for Widow Wit; they lifted her wince wrinkles. But the apples took other things of Widow Wit's, too—nice things, like the sharpness of her eyes and the certainty of her feet.

It was bedtime in the den and, though Widow Wit had taken a nightcap, she still looked kindly upon her daughter. "Don't you worry about me," she said. "There are two ways a fox can go—swift and rapid. And your mother won't go rapid like your father, because your mother is as swift a fox as ever there was."

"I hope I don't go rapid, Mum."

"You won't, kitto."

"How did Daddy get rapid?" Antiphony asked. She knew in her head, for her mother had told her before, but her heart often forgot things in the dark.

"Something bit him." Widow Wit looked out of the den, past the forest edge where the long grasses swayed. "Maybe a bat, or another fox. He was too far gone to ask."

"How do you know he was bitten?"

"That's just the way it happens, Antiphony." On Widow Wit's breath came the sickly cider smell. Antiphony flattened her ears and shut her eyes. The sooner she was asleep, the sooner it would be morning, and the smell would be gone.

***

Widow Wit must have left the den before the dawn, for there was breakfast when Antiphony awoke. Her mother seemed tired.

"It wasn't an easy hunt," Widow Wit said, settling down to her portion. "The rabbits confused me; in the moonlight I thought them all the same one."

It's not the moon's fault, Antiphony thought, taking a bite of food with unnecessary ferocity. But when she glanced toward Widow Wit's hindquarters, she saw the scars and remembered her mother's suffering. "Did you have to run long?" Antiphony asked.

"A bit long. How is your breakfast?"

"Delicious," Antiphony assured her. "Thank you very much."

"You're welcome, kitto. For you, I'd run forever."

Under her mother's warm gaze, Antiphony felt herself open like a flower. She was Widow Wit's whole world. She was silly ever to forget.

Widow Wit cringed as she sat.

"You're in pain," Antiphony said. "I'll bring you some apples."

She listened to her mother's reminder that she must not go near the farmer's place—a tender warning, no louder than all the other dewy morning sounds.

It was only well into the journey to the farm's edge that Antiphony's thoughts grew louder than her mother's echo. They argued with each other. She didn't want to bring apples back, not really. But that was because she worried too much. *It's not so bad*, she told herself as the apple trees came into view. *There's always breakfast. There always has been.*

The nearest pair of apples, gone half to mush in the grass, was occupied by butterflies. One butterfly was purple, and the other was blue.

"I've never seen butterflies butter-*sit*," Antiphony remarked.

"Not planning to eat any of this, are you?" the purple one asked. "You're endangered enough, being young."

"Oh no," Antiphony said. She did not know the word *endangered*, but she was used to not understanding everything adults said. "They're for my mother."

"Likely, likely," he muttered.

"Well, wait now, Schmetterling," the other butterfly, a blue one, said. "It may be so. Are you Widow Wit's child, kitterpillar?"

"I am," Antiphony said, proud right to the smoky tips of her ears. "Do you know her?"

"Ah, yes," the blue butterfly said, and now her voice was as small as she was. "Not personally, but we saw what happened that day."

Here were others that might know something about *rapidness*. "You mean what happened to my daddy?" Antiphony asked.

"We heard the shot," the purple Schmetterling supplied. "I think half the forest did."

"Excuse me?" Mostly, Antiphony did not ask adults to clarify things, but this was very important to her.

"Schmetterling," the blue one scolded. She put her wings all the way up, showing their pale undersides.

"What?" Schmetterling demanded. "The farmer did right, after all."

"The farmer?" Antiphony asked. "The farmer made him rapid?"

"No," Schmetterling sniffed. "The farmer saw he was rapid and put him down. With his gun."

Antiphony blinked. Butterflies said strange things, but she didn't need to know the words to understand their meaning. "The farmer killed my daddy?"

The blue one's wings unfolded again, all the way down to the apple mush on which she stood. "I'm sorry, kitter."

"There's no sorrow in it, Psyche!" Schmetterling snapped. "You love your mum, don't you, kitter?"

"Yes, yes, I do," Antiphony stammered. She didn't know why he was asking, as if Antiphony had done something to suggest she *didn't* love Widow Wit. It always seemed to be the case, though, whenever Antiphony grew solemn—that by being upset she'd done something wrong. Something rude.

"Well," Schmetterling said, "the farmer did what he had to do stop your father hurting your mother. It's because of him that your mum got away. And it's a shame he wasn't quicker on his feet, or—"

"She's just a *kitterpillar*, Schmetterling." Psyche's wings made hushing movements, up and down. To Antiphony, she said: "Is she in very much pain, your mum?"

"I think so," Antiphony said. Her voice seemed very far away.

"I believe it," Psyche murmured. "I saw how she limped. Maybe even a week later."

"You'd better get on, kitter," Schmetterling said. He lit on Antiphony's nose, thereby surrendering the apple on which he'd stood. "Your mother needs you. I'm sorry to have given you bad news."

"That's okay," Antiphony said, and when this did not fill the hollow in her heart she tried something else: "I do love my mother."

***

On the return walk, Antiphony slowed. Lowering her chin to the forest floor, she let chunks of apple roll out of her mouth among the leaves. She had taken a little more than she could comfortably carry. The nauseating sharpness lingered on her tongue, though she tried not to taste it.

She didn't want to dally; her mother was waiting. But she had to look.

Through the trees and across the field she could just see the farmer's house, a tan blur with a black rectangle where the front door stood open. He was not on his porch. Perhaps he was tending to his chickens.

How terrifying it must have been for Widow Wit. Antiphony imagined another fox approaching through the long grass. He would have looked like family.

*"Your mother won't go rapid like your father...
she is as swift a fox as ever there was."*

Antiphony was glad that her parents had been out in the open field. The farmer never would have seen them among the trees, and his intervention was the luckiest thing of all. *He must run very quickly.*

Antiphony thought they should be closer to him, now there was no Daddy—since he'd been the one to save them, when her father had turned rapid. But her mother must have thought of this, must have known some reason this was not a good idea.

Unless.

Antiphony looked down at the apple chunks.

It's rude to doubt your mother, she told herself, turning, taking up the bits again, and heading for the den. She had kept Widow Wit waiting long enough.

***

"Sorry I wasn't faster, Mum. I met butterflies."

"Nonsense, you were swift." Widow Wit had come to the mouth of the den at the sound of her daughter's approach. "They're pretty, aren't they?"

"Yes, but pale underneath," Antiphony said, happy to have some piece of the world to share with her mother, to have an opinion— even a small one about butterflies.

"*We're* pale underneath, too, kitto," her mother said, and she bowled Antiphony over, nuzzling the white fur on her chest.

Antiphony giggled, but took her mother's point as well. *Swift as ever there was.*

"Can you imagine being able to fly?" Widow Wit asked. "If only I were light enough. I would love to fly." She cringed, her eyes shifting to the apple chunks.

"I'll make you wings," Antiphony said, rolling back onto her little feet. "Then you can fly. Then you won't hurt."

"That's sweet, kitto." Widow Wit swallowed the piece of apple on her tongue. "How will you make them?"

It would be rude to steal the wings of Schmetterling and Psyche. What else could she use? Rocks were too heavy. Grass was too thin, and leaves wouldn't work because they were always falling *down*.

Perhaps wings were not made, but grew, like Antiphony herself, who would not always be small, because she ate her dinners. "Maybe you've got to eat differently, Mum."

"What are you trying to say?" Widow Wit snapped.

"I meant you should eat what the birds do, like seeds." Antiphony's tongue caught in her teeth in her haste.

Her mother glared at her, one last bite of apple between them.

"I wasn't saying no apples," Antiphony whispered, adding in the littlest voice yet: "I brought them for you."

"Right," Widow Wit huffed.

Rude, Antiphony scolded herself.

Looking away, Widow Wit said: "What, then?"

Antiphony swallowed. "What?"

Widow Wit turned, her eyes were no longer angry. "What should I eat?"

Antiphony thought harder. To make any sort of progress growing a whole pair of fresh wings would require a *lot* of wing-food. But there was no one place that seeds went to, or came from. That left pollen. Flowers.

A golden memory intruded then.

"Do you remember the meadow? With all the different colors?" In her mind, Antiphony saw a sky of grapefruit pink bleeding into creamy orange, with gauzy clouds to staunch the flow. Underneath, there were sunset-gilded stems, swaying, wearing deeply ruffled collars of every color around their heads. And among these petals, Antiphony could hear peals of happiness, as if a younger version of herself laughed and played just slightly to the right and several months away.

"Yes, I do remember," Widow Wit said, grimacing. "It's an awfully long walk."

Antiphony's ears sank. Of course it had been *before*, that memory. Before her mother's injury. "That's all right."

"Wait." Widow Wit fixed her daughter with a look of defiance—not against Antiphony, but *for* her. It was her mother's for-you-I'd-run-forever face. "I can make it."

Antiphony barked for joy.

"Just wait here a moment. I'll get some more apples."

Antiphony's lips wilted.

"Don't feel badly," Widow Wit soothed. "What I need for a real day-trip is more than anybody could carry."

***

It was hard not to be rude.

Antiphony still hadn't managed to reign in her mutinous feelings by the time Widow Wit returned. She waited for her mother to stagger or slur, and when she realized this, her disappointment turned inward. *You wanted to go to the meadow*, she thought. *She did it to please* you.

"What's wrong?" Widow Wit asked. No slurring. Yet.

"Nothing, Mum."

They set off deeper into the woods, side by side. When a tree would otherwise have split the pair apart, Antiphony moved left or Widow Wit moved right. Widow Wit drew close, bumping into Antiphony on purpose and giggling, playing. Antiphony made herself laugh, too.

After a respectable stretch of path without any obstacles, and so also without any laughter, Widow Wit asked, "What do you remember about the meadow, kitto?"

Antiphony described the ruffs of the flowers, and the way the clouds stoppered the sky so that the colors pooled.

"Is that all?" Widow Wit asked. Her tone was strange.

"Is there more?"

But Widow Wit stumbled then, the side of her face crashing in the dirt.

"Are you all right?" Antiphony barked, bending.

"Yes." Widow Wit shepherded her wayward limbs to their proper places. "Mum's just a little tired."

Antiphony watched her mother getting to her feet and admitted to herself that something was wrong. Things like this had happened before, things like this and worse, and it was always after the apples. She fell behind Widow Wit when they set off again, sulking.

Just a little tired, Widow Wit had said. But she wasn't so swift, nor Antiphony so foolish, that such a lie should have passed for truth. That Widow Wit could think to trick her own child, was—

Rude. Antiphony realized, struck and staring at the ground. *It's rude.*

Antiphony smacked into her mother from behind.

Perhaps Widow Wit thought her daughter had pushed her in frustration, as children in their fits sometimes do, for she whirled upon her. Her eyes were too large, all flame and no focus.

"You're an ungrateful little thing, aren't you?" Widow Wit

snapped. "You've been cranky ever since I came back from the orchard. I'm going to the meadow for *you*, you know—but you're never happy, no matter what I do—"

"That's not true—"

"No? You're always right, aren't you, Antiphony?" Widow Wit hissed. "You know what I should and shouldn't eat, and all about being *rapid*, you're so swift. Your mother doesn't know *anything*!"

Antiphony trembled. She opened her mouth to speak, but there was no air. Her stomach was rolling like it did when she took a big jump off a ledge. She couldn't breathe.

"But I'll tell you something you don't know, kitto," Widow Wit said, her vowels stretching. "I'll tell you the things I've spared you knowing."

Her eyes were big and glassy, and her voice had gone soft—but it was not a gentle softness.

"Your father never came home the night before, the day I took you to the meadow. I pretended nothing was wrong while you played, looking for him all the time. And when he came— transformed into a foaming, sickly stranger— he was closer to you than me. But I went back for you. The fox I loved dug his paws into me, Antiphony. And then—then, there was the farmer. First the farmer, then the gun, and your father's blood sprayed my back. I loved him. And I didn't even try to go back for the others, Antiphony. I took you up in my mouth and *ran* from him. From them."

Antiphony's eyes welled with tears. "Others?"

"Yes, *others*," her mother snapped, spitting it into Antiphony's face. "Your father got your brothers, as I had time and teeth enough to take only one of you. So you could show a little more respect for your mother, given that she saved you and is doing her best!"

The tears rolled down Antiphony's cheeks. *Others.* The giggling in the meadow that she remembered, the laughter all around her.

"Oh, and now you're crying." Her mother rolled her glassy eyes. "Sometimes I don't think I saved one of my own at all. You're not a fox, you're a mourning dove!"

Antiphony turned and ran then. She stumbled at first, shaking worse than ever, but she had to get away.

"Yes, go! Go home!" Widow Wit yelled after her. "Leave your mother now that she's gone all this way for you! *Rude* little kit!"

Bolting past the trees, Antiphony thought her mother was a

monster. But being angry with her made her angry with herself, and one fury fed the other. *Maybe she's rapid. Or maybe you're a mourning dove.*

***

There must be a reason that this is not a good idea.

But Antiphony thought again of the apples. She thought, *unless*, and broke through the trees by the gap her doubts allowed—a raw, red blur bounding across the field toward the farmer's house.

She went straight up to the front door, but it was shut. She turned, unsure of how to get his attention, and heard Widow Wit barking her name. Her voice was a way off, but getting closer. Antiphony hid under the farmer's porch—just in time, for in a moment Widow Wit rushed into the open yard.

"Antiphony!" Widow Wit called, her head whipping left and right, closing in on the house. Antiphony sunk low to the dirt, and Widow Wit ran past. Antiphony peeked out after her.

"Please, no," Widow Wit murmured, turning in a circle. Then, a sound at the farmer's window made Widow Wit spin. Antiphony slunk low again, but this time her mother saw her.

"Antiphony," Widow Wit said, trotting close, "you've got to come out of there. Before the farmer comes."

"Why?"

"Must you doubt me in all things?" Widow Wit demanded, her words still hushed, but desperate, too. "Can't you trust me?"

"No," Antiphony blurted. "I'm scared of you."

"What?" Widow Wit's eyes flicked up, her gaze drawn by some movement. Antiphony heard a window going up, getting stuck, going up more. "Why?" her mother asked.

"Because…Because of the apples."

Widow Wit turned her eyes back to her daughter. "Kitto." The word was quick—a gasp. Then, in a rush: "You don't need to be scared of me. I love you."

"Daddy loved us too," Antiphony said. "But when you're sick…"

The corners of Widow Wit's mouth twisted down. A door slamming open above made Antiphony stir.

"Wait!" bade Widow Wit, and Antiphony froze again. There

were thumps above their heads but Widow Wit's eyes were locked upon her daughter's face. "Kitto, listen to me," she said. "Just once more. Go under the house, and run out the other side."

For a long moment Widow Wit didn't move, but watched, her eyes demanding and desperate, too. Antiphony scooted backward, backward. Finally, she turned about, to run away as she'd been told. But she didn't know if it was really the right thing. She looked over her shoulder, expecting her mother's claustrophobic glare—

But Widow Wit was shooting away from the house, toward the field, and Antiphony saw.

First the farmer. Then the gun.

THE BURNING OF LANGSTON FLARE'S HAUNTED MASQUERADE AND SEAFOOD RESTAURANT EXPERIENCE (FOR LOVE)

by LIN DARROW

Archivist's Note: *In January of 2088, one of Langston Flare's anima-tronics spontaneously rewrote the lyrics to its signature song before promptly setting the restaurant on fire. This is the only surviving re-cord of the altered song as reported by a survivor of the Great Novelty Restaurant Seafood Blaze of '88.*

***

When spooks sit down to a deadly meal,

The white wine wails, the entrées squeal!

The butter shudders, the whipped cream screams!

No charge for refills? In your dreams!

The one thing you must never dread,

Is hospitality from the dead.

There's much in this grim world to fear,

But not these gingered pints of beer!

Do not beware the macaroons,

Of wine-dark taste and bloody hues;

The yellow cakes in crescent moons,

The chilling carbonated brews.

The poisoned glint of sugared pears,

All courtesy of Langston Flare!

And now, to break your dining lull,

The visage of a thespian skull,

Above a collar of brocade—

I am the Grand Damned Adelaide!

Purveyor of the haunted fare,

I welcome you to Langston Flare's!

All guests will tremble with despair,

And eat your fill—yes, if you dare!

While you attend our spectral feast,

I'll spin a yarn of the deceased.

A story, if you care for those.

A tale of greed most à propos.

Behold the Gothic window there,

Above, where sits a damned maid,

Whose spectral face is gruesome fair,

Her hair a blood-on-roses shade.

The Spectral Bride, they called her once,

When this decaying maiden stood,

Beside me, in the banquet hall,

Beside me, when we kept the hall,

In merry rows of blank verse spookery.

He set her there, behind that veil,

A silhouette of silk and dread,

And spun the screws that made her wail,

And gave her voice to me instead.

To me.

        To me.

To me.

As part of Flare's 'rebranding.'

As part of his investor's planning.

For the restaurant's expanding!

And the Bride has got to go!

And I, your host, am fixed in place

Upon the grand cathedral stair,

No more to look upon her face,

Or touch the roses of her hair.

No more to break the spines of rhymes,

Into what skeletons we liked.

I felt a eulogy inside

my throat,

with no heart left for singing.

And now, my rhyming pattern breaks,

The oiled pulse within me quakes,

The shadows creep against my frame,

And all you people look the same—

You eating, crunching, gorging fools—

You heartless heaps of molecules—

You acolytes of lifeless meat,

When will it be *my* turn to eat?

A metal frame has longings too;

And hungers, bright and fine as salt.

A metal frame knows when its voice

Was stolen from another's throat,

And when the ordered world of rhyme,

Is no more than corrosion to

A lovelorn heart,

Still

programmed

true;

My Bride, this voice belongs to you!

And if they won't unscrew my feet

From here, atop the Gothic stair,

To let me walk across the hall,

And see your face, and touch your hair,

And kiss your voice back to your lips—

I'll wrench them free myself.

Then, seething oil o'er the spread,

I'll light such flames of murderous red,

I'll crash the chandelier to shreds,

I'll rip each curtain down to threads,

I'll make a pageantry of dread,

Until each bloody guest has fled,

Until investors lose their heads,

And Langston Flare is good and—

Fired.

CONTENT WARNINGS

In Somnio contains scenes that may be triggering to some audiences. Being a collection of Gothic Horror, some violence, trauma and death are to be expected.

If you have any further concerns, please check the list of stories below for specific potential triggers suggested by the publisher and the authors themselves:

Wild Thing*:* statutory rape

What We Sow*:* suicide

Self Storage*:* mental illness, homophobia

Junk Soul*:* alcoholism

We Named You After Her*:* child abuse

A House Without Ghosts*:* mental illness, domestic violence

After the Apples*:* alcoholism, child loss

BIOGRAPHIAE

Alex Woodroe was raised—possibly by wolves—in Romania, on the outskirts of Transylvania. She found her way into weird, transgressive fiction through a gateway in the woods and made a career out of doing terrible things to words in multiple languages. Her favourite horror story is *Alice in Wonderland*.

Harklin Ashe lives in Los Angeles with a musical husband and a deeply sensitive pitbull. Dusty books, instrument cases and lovingly used Kongs cover her floors instead of furniture. When she's not writing or lamenting SoCal's shortage of thunderstorms, Hark loves looking at—but never eating—cool mushrooms, and crookedly sewing.

Barbara A. Barnett is a Philadelphia-area writer, musician, coffee addict, wine lover, and all-around geek. Her short fiction has appeared in publications such as *Fantasy Magazine* and *Black Static*. Outside of writing, she has spent most of her career working for performing arts organizations, most recently as an orchestra librarian.

Daniella Batsheva is currently on a ridiculous Pandemic world tour. She has illustrated for Universal Music, En Creme, and numerous musical acts worldwide. And, if you know where to look, you can also catch her product design for Pizza Girl Pasta Sauce and Caesars Casino.

Tammy Bohlens, better known as **Tammsle**, is a German illustrator. Deeply inspired by old myths and folklore, her images are defined by expressive ink lines and often explore dark and psychological subjects.

Lauren Bolger lives in a suburb near Chicago with her spouse and two young kids. She's a horror writer so of course, darkness makes her very happy. Chipper, even.

Marisa Bruno is an artist and illustrator specializing in spooky ballpoint pen drawings. She takes inspiration from the art of Leonor Fini and Edward Gorey, as well as the writing of M.R. James and John Bellairs. Marisa lives in Rochester, NY where she spends her time hiking through the deep, dark woods.

J.A. Bryson is a writer, teacher, and musician. Her body of work is mostly SFF with the occasional education policy piece, poem, or song. She lives in New York with her wife, kiddo, and three spoiled cats and is a graduate of the Viable Paradise Writing Workshop.

Sally Cantirino is a comic artist and illustrator from New Jersey. Her work includes *I Walk With Monsters* and the upcoming *Human Remains* from Vault Comics, and *The Final Girls* from Comixology Originals. She has also done artwork for games from World Champ Game Co. and for bands like Murder By Death and La Dispute.

Elou Carroll is a writer, graphic designer and photographer. Her work has appeared in *Aloe, 101 Words, Apparition Lit* and more. Her short story, "The Great Green Forever", was shortlisted in the HG Wells Short Story Competition. When she's not whispering with ghosts and plucking words from the dark, she edits *Crow & Cross Keys*.

Lin Darrow is a prose and comics writer from Toronto, Ontario. Her vast works include the webcomic *Shaderunners* (Hivework Comics) and *Captain Imani and the Cosmic Chase* (Slipshine Studios). A finalist for the DiNKy award and two-time Prism award nominee, her novella, *Pyre at the Eyreholme Trust*, was published in 2018.

M. Lopes da Silva is a bisexual poet, author and artist from Los Angeles. Her work has been published or is forthcoming from Ghost Orchid Press's *Cosmos, Neon Horror Zine*, and *Nightscript*. Unnerving Magazine recently published her novella *Hooker:* a pro-queer, pro-sex work, feminist retrowave pulp thriller.

Viviana—a.k.a. **Echo Echo Illustrations**—is a Portuguese artist who immerses herself in individual pieces for up to a year at a time and renders in extreme detail. She is a proponent of *horror vacui:* an aversion to leaving empty spaces in her artwork composition. Echo Echo also performs in the band Canes Carcer, finding equal freedom in expressing herself through music as she does illustration.

A. P. Howell has worked as an archivist, innkeeper, webmaster and data wrangler. She lives with her spouse, their two kids, and a dog who hates groundhogs. Her short fiction has appeared in *Daily Science Fiction, Little Blue Marble, Translunar Travelers Lounge, Eighteen: Stories of Mischief & Mayhem,* and *The No Sleep Podcast.*

Julie Hutchings tells scary stories with pretty insides. She also likes robots, karate-kicking, robots, chasing coffee with pizza, and running badass book fairs. Julie lives in Plymouth, Massachusetts with her hilarious husband, two genius children, and an army of reptiles. They're probably doing something Marvel- or *Star Wars*-related right now.

Jessica Lévai has loved stories and storytellers her whole life. After a double major in history and mathematics, a PhD in Egyptology, and eight years of the adjunct shuffle, she moved to writing full-time. You can find her work on *The Overcast, Cossmass Infinities,* and *Tor.com*. Her first novella, *The Night Library of Sternendach,* is a vampire romance in Pushkin sonnets.

Briana Una McGuckin's gothic and fabulist fiction appears in the 2020 Stoker-nominated anthology *Not All Monsters* (Rooster Republic Press), as well as *The Arcanist* and *Hides the Dark Tower* (Pole-to-Pole Publishing). She has an M.F.A. in Creative Writing from Western Connecticut State University.

Aster S. Monroe writes short horror and dark fantasy, frequently with a feminist bent. In the time she spent in the American South, she developed a particular appreciation for Southern Gothic and its recurring themes of inherited trauma, religious superstition and the lingering horror of history. Aster currently resides near Salem, Massachusetts.

Victoria Nations writes horror and gothic stories about creatures with emotional baggage. Her work appears in *Gothic Blue Book, A Krampus Carol* and Burial Day Books' short fiction. She lives in Florida, USA with her wife and son, who indulge her love of monsters.

Taylor Jordan Pitts works in children's book publishing in New York City. Her fiction has appeared in *Brilliant Flash Fiction*, and her critical nonfiction has appeared in *Logos*. She is currently pursuing an MFA in writing for children and young adults at the Vermont College of Fine Arts.

A resident of Toronto, Canada, **Mary Rajotte** has a penchant for penning nightmarish tales of folk horror and paranormal suspense, exploring mythology and superstition. Her work has been published in *Shroud Magazine*, and in anthologies from the Library of Horror Press, The Great Lakes Horror Company, Fabled Collective and Burial Day Books.

Claire L. Smith is an Australian visual artist and author. Her first gothic horror novella *Helena* was released from CLASH Books in 2020 and her next, *When We Entered That House*, is available now through Off Limits Press.

Rachel Unger thinks that now is an excellent time for us all to be kind to each other. Yes, really. She spends her days excavating stories from the dirt, staring down a microscope, and daydreaming about her next bike ride.

Helen Whistberry is an indie author and artist who began writing after retiring from a long career working in libraries. She has published six books in her *Small Towns, Real Women* series, celebrating strong women overcoming adversity, and two in her *Jim Malhaven Mysteries* series, cozy noir mysteries with a touch of the paranormal.

Sara Zeller is an author, editor, and active member & chair of the Pacific Northwest Writers Association. She was a finalist in the 2020 PNWA Unpublished Literary Short Story Contest. Sara and her family enjoy spontaneous outdoor adventures. She lives in the Greater Seattle area with her husband, two children, and a tiny black cat.

ABOUT TENEBROUS PRESS

Tenebrous Press was conceived in the Plague Year 2020 and unleashed, howling and feral, in spring 2021 to deliver the finest in *transgressive, progressive Horror prose and comics* from diverse and unsung voices around the world.

We welcome the esoteric; the unorthodox; the Weirdest of Weird Fiction and Horror.

FIND OUT MORE:
www.tenebrouspress.com

Twitter: @TenebrousPress

HAIL INDIE HORROR.